Maisey Yates is a *New York Times* bestselling author of over seventy-five romance novels. She has a coffee habit she has no interest in kicking, and a slight Pinterest addiction. She lives with her husband and children in the Pacific Northwest. When Maisey isn't writing she can be found singing in the grocery store, shopping for shoes online and probably not doing dishes. Check out her website: maiseyyates.com.

CROWNED FOR MY ROYAL BABY

MAISEY YATES

MILLS & BOON

First Published in Great Britain 2020
by Mills & Boon, an imprint of HarperCollins*Publishers*
1 London Bridge Street, London, SE1 9GF

ISBN: 978-0-263-08874-8

MIX
Paper from
responsible sources
FSC® C007454

This book is produced from independently certified FSC™ paper
to ensure responsible forest management.
For more information visit www.harpercollins.co.uk/green.

Printed and bound in Great Britain
by CPI Group (UK) Ltd, Croydon, CR0 4YY

To the librarians.
And mine especially.
At school and at the public library.
You made sure I had books. Lots of books. All the books.
If not for my love of reading, I'm sure I wouldn't be writing.
Thank you.

CHAPTER ONE

Marissa

I'LL NEVER FORGET the first time I saw Prince Hercules. A ridiculous name, and one more suited to a bronzed god than a man. The kind of god my father would have called a false one and told me to steer clear of.

If he could only have known. He would have locked me in my room for the foreseeable future if he'd had any real idea of how fallible I was.

Something in me must have known.

Because Hercules immediately became a secret. Even when I watched him from a distance.

Secrets were not allowed in my family because a secret meant that someone was concealing a truth. And if you were concealing a truth, it had to be because it was a sin.

Hercules became sin for me very, very quickly.

It was after church that first time. I had gone down to the water, as I often did on the small island of Medland, Massachusetts.

It was summer, and the elite had already descended on the tiny town as they did every year. The influx of seasonal residents as welcome as they were overwhelming.

The island ran on summer business, the money made during those months often necessarily hoarded through the rest of the year.

The collection plates at my father's church were certainly fuller during those weeks.

And while I knew, even at sixteen, that the rush of people was necessary for the economy, I still found it overwhelming.

And so I retreated, not to the most heaving parts of the beaches, but to private paths that beat through tall seagrass and down to rocky but tranquil shores that were far too rustic to attract the volume of visitors the vast stretches of sand did.

On a Saturday it was difficult to find spaces that weren't overrun, but I'd lived there all my life and barely knew anywhere else. I knew where I could find solitude if I wanted it.

And that was where I first spotted him.

He was standing in the waves, the water lapping at his knees, his pants rolled up, his shirt off.

He was surrounded by people—women specifically—laughing and chatting, splashing each other. But he stood out, his face looking like it was carved from granite.

His eyes reminded me of obsidian. The black glossy rock that both gave off light and consumed it all at once. I thought I could get lost in those eyes.

In that darkness.

I'd been taught to run from darkness, but there was a

glow in his I couldn't turn away from. I felt like I'd just discovered a creature I wasn't allowed to know existed.

He seemed lost in whatever his darkness was.

Until one of the women touched his arm, and those features shifted into a smile that seemed to eclipse the sun. And I was suddenly overcome by a strange, bitter taste in my mouth that I'd never experienced before. It made my whole body feel tight and strange.

I ran away.

But the next day, I went back after church, and he was there. This time, not out in the water, but standing on the shore.

And he saw me.

"Are you going to stare all day?" he asked.

"I wasn't staring at you," I replied. "I was simply taking in the view behind you."

"I saw you yesterday," he said. "On the shore." The way he said it made it clear he didn't believe I was looking at anything but him. "You ran away."

"I knew my father would wonder where I was. You weren't in church today?" I asked him. An inane question. I knew he wasn't there. I would have noticed. Everyone would have.

"No," he said with a laugh. "I find my worship, such as it might be, is best conducted outside four walls. And you?"

"My father is the pastor. I'll get in trouble if I don't go."

"And would you get in trouble if he found out you were here?"

He was even more beautiful up close. His chest was covered then, thank God, or I probably would have expired on the spot. It was a weakness, I knew, the way that I looked at him. The way that I hungrily took in every inch of bronze skin that was on display. Just a wedge, where the fabric of his white shirt was separated.

I knew that I was wicked.

Like a sudden answer to my restlessness had locked into place and printed the definition in my brain.

Wicked.

It was evidenced in the way I feasted on every detail of his handsome, sculpted face. But I couldn't help it, and for the first time, I didn't want to.

He looked familiar, but I couldn't place him. That square, sharp jaw and compelling mouth, those dark, intense eyes.

"Possibly," I said. "I'm supposed to be careful about talking to... Well, most people who come here during the summer are very important. And also...of a certain sort of character."

"Whoremongers and the like?" he asked, a glint of humor in his eyes.

I felt my cheeks heat. "I suppose so."

"Sadly, I'm both," he said. "You should probably run away."

"Okay," I said and instantly turned to flee, doing exactly as I was told, because I didn't know another way to be.

"Do you always do what people tell you to?" he asked me, stopping me in my tracks.

"I... Yes."

"You should stop that. Figure out what you want."

"I'll probably just get a job here. Get married." Just

mentioning that word in front of him made my insides feel jittery.

He arched a brow. "But is it what you want?"

He was looking at me so intently, and I couldn't for the life of me figure out why a man such as him would look at a girl like me the way that he was.

Of course, I didn't exactly know what the look was. I had never spoken to a man I didn't know from church. Not outside of exchanged pleasantries on a street. We didn't even know each other.

I didn't know his name, and he didn't know mine.

He was an admitted whoremonger, and someone very important. And there I was, talking to him anyway. Feeling pinned to the spot by all that intensity.

"I've never thought about it," I finally admitted.

"Do," he said. "And get back to me."

I didn't see him for the next few days, but I was consumed by schoolwork anyway. It was summer, but as I was homeschooled, my parents didn't much acknowledge breaks. It was fine, because I was on the verge of graduating at sixteen, though to what end, I didn't know. I had considered going away for a while on a mission, which was something that my parents heartily approved of.

I went back to check on Saturday again to see if I could find the mystery man.

I didn't.

But I did again, that next Sunday.

"Have you thought about what you want?" he asked.

I just stared at him blankly, because no, I hadn't. I had thought about him. And that was it.

That began a strange sort of friendship. We would

talk by the seashore when he was alone. About every-thing and nothing. Not about ourselves, but the world.

He'd been everywhere, and I'd been nowhere. We both found that fascinating.

We didn't exchange names. He gave me a seashell, and he told me that the way it swirled at the center re-minded him of the way my hair curled. I put it in a box and hid it under my bed.

When the summer ended, I couldn't breathe.

He was gone and the world was gray. It was silly to grieve over a man who was alive, but not with me. A man whose name I didn't know.

But I grieved all the same.

Sometime in the middle of winter a photograph on the front page of a tabloid in the grocery store caught my eye—it was him. It was him with a beautiful woman on his arm and his name plastered right there on the newsprint, and I had to ask myself how I could be so stupid.

I wasn't one to pay attention to popular culture—in fact, my father expressly forbade it—and often I averted my eyes even when waiting in the checkout line, so there was a certain sort of sense in the fact that I hadn't realized immediately who my seaside friend was.

Not just someone important.

A *prince*.

Prince Hercules Xenakis of Pelion, one of the most renowned playboys in the entire world.

That night I took the box out from under my bed and stared at the seashell, and I told myself I should get rid of it.

He wouldn't be coming back to the island—I was certain of it.

I would never see him again. Our meeting—our friendship—had been a fluke, and what was more, I was sure that I meant nothing to him. I was a schoolgirl, a common one at that, and he was one of the most wealthy, desirable men on the planet.

I couldn't bring myself to throw it away.

Summer rolled around, marking my birthday and marking the return of the seasonal residents.

And there he was.

Sunday afternoon.

I told myself not to smile like a giddy fool when I saw him, but I did. And he smiled at me.

"You're still here," he said, shoving his hands in his pockets.

"I live here. So it's not truly that surprising. You came back," I said. I looked away from him. "You're a prince."

"Ah," he said. "So you've discovered my secret." He sounded regretful.

I peered at him while still trying to keep my head tilted down. "I'm not sure how it can be a secret, given you are frequently on the cover of newspapers."

He touched me then. His fingertips brushed my chin, and I lifted my head, my eyes meeting his. The impact left me breathless. "Does that change things?"

I was stunned. "Doesn't it have to?"

"I don't think so," he said. "I knew I was a prince this whole time. And anyway, that you didn't is part of why I liked spending time with you."

I held that close for the rest of the week.

He liked me. He liked me because I didn't know he was a prince, and he didn't think I was a fool.

That next week I told him my name. "Marissa," I said. "Since I know yours."

"Yes, it's quite a difficult name to use in conversation, don't you think?"

"I assume that's helped by the fact that most people probably call you by an honorific."

"Indeed. But I would rather you did not."

"Hercules?" His name tasted strange on my lips, and not just because it was foreign.

"Yes," he said, smiling at me.

"Then I will."

I knew he was older than me, richer than me, more experienced than me, impossible in every way. But in that moment, as his smile lit his face, I fell in love with him.

He gave me another seashell, and I thought maybe he might feel something for me.

When he went away that summer, I couldn't help but follow the headlines about him. I made myself sick with them.

Because there he was, with beautiful women on his arm, and if he felt for me even a fraction of what I did for him, there was no way that he would be with them. I bought an entertainment magazine with his picture on it, and I knew that if my father found it, I would be in trouble. I put it in the box with the seashells. I felt guilty, because now I had secrets.

Now I didn't do what I was told.

I seemed to do things because of Hercules instead, and that was something entirely different.

I finished school, but I didn't want to go away on a mission trip, because he would be coming back. So I made an excuse about wanting a job, got one at a local coffeehouse called the Snowy Owl.

And mostly, I lived for Sundays.

Of course, nobody scheduled me to work on a Sunday, because my father would forbid that I do anything on the Sabbath.

I didn't care about that. I cared about him.

"You're back," I said to him. First thing, just as I had done the year before.

I was eighteen, and I burned with a strange kind of conviction in my chest, because I didn't feel quite so helpless. Quite like there was such a barrier between us.

Oh sure, there was the Prince thing. The fact that he spent the year dating supermodels and traveling around on private jets. But I was a woman now. And I felt like that had to mean something.

"Of course."

"I'm glad," I said.

"So am I."

Then he reached out his hand and took hold of mine. "Shall we go for a walk?"

"Yes," I said.

And for the first time, I held a man's hand. His fingers were so warm, and it made my stomach turn over, made my heart feel like it was going to race right out of my chest. I looked at him, and he looked completely unaffected, but he still held on to me, and so I held on to that.

He kissed me on one of those Sunday afternoons.

My whole body felt like it would burst into flame.

His lips were firm and sure on mine, and he was so impossibly beautiful.

Every feeling he called up in me I had been taught to identify as a sin, but it was so beautiful, and part of him, and I couldn't bring myself to turn away from it.

So instead, I wrapped my arms around him and kissed him back. Parted my lips for him and allowed him to brush his tongue against mine.

I allowed all kinds of things on those Sunday afternoons. For his touch to become more familiar. For the feeling of his body against mine to become the dearest and most precious thing in the world. All that hard, powerful muscle, gentled as he held me.

I wanted to tell him he didn't have to leash that strength. But I didn't have the words for it. I didn't have the vocabulary for what I wanted at all.

"Can you meet me tonight?"

It was near the end of summer when he asked me that, and I wanted to. Desperately. But I knew that I would get in so much trouble if I were caught.

Do you always do what you're told?

That earlier question came back to haunt me. And no, I didn't do what I was told. Not anymore. Not now.

I lived for Hercules.

It wasn't about whether I might marry him and become a princess. I never thought about the future. I only thought about us, as we were, there on the beach. His life outside of that didn't matter, and neither did mine.

And so I made the decision to expand it. To push outside those isolated Sunday afternoons and see something more.

"Yes."

I climbed out my window that night and met him there at our spot, in the darkness. He had a blanket and a bottle of wine, and I had never tried alcohol before. I declined the wine, but I got drunk on his mouth, on his touch. And before I knew it, things had gone much further than I had intended.

It went on like that over the weeks, until I didn't care anymore what was supposed to be right. The only thing that felt right was being in his arms. And when I gave him my virginity, I gave it easily, joyously. And he showed me what pleasure meant, and why people jumped into ruin with careless abandon and joy in their hearts.

It was the night he left that it happened.

He had to go. He couldn't stay away from home any longer.

He didn't ask me to go with him.

I told myself he couldn't.

He and I forgot everything. We made love on a blanket in the sand until neither of us could breathe, and it wasn't until later that I realized he'd forgotten protection of any kind.

He was gone the next day.

And three weeks later I knew my life had changed forever.

I had no idea how to begin contacting the palace.

But that wasn't even what worried me, not right at first. It was telling my parents. But I knew that I had to call Hercules first.

I knew you couldn't just call up a palace. Still, I had to try.

I called the palace directory. I left a message. I heard nothing.

I called again. Again and again.

Finally, in my desperation I told the person on the other end of the line that I had to get in touch with Prince Hercules, since I was having his baby.

The next day, men in suits came to the coffeehouse.

They whisked me into the manager's office, and they told me that I was never to reach out to Hercules again. And that if I agreed to sign stacks of thick legal documents and never reveal the paternity of my child, I would be given enough money to live more than comfortably forever.

My heart shattered into pieces. Desperate, enraged, I threw the papers and ran. I ran all the way back home.

My secret burst out of me. Flowing like the tears that were pouring down my face. I admitted to my parents that I was pregnant.

My father's face turned to stone. He asked if I intended to marry the father of my child, and quickly. I told him I could not, because he had abandoned me.

He didn't have to say anything. His face said it all. He had warned me. He had told me. And I had failed. I was wicked, just like the rest of them. And that was when he told me he would have to wash his hands of me. Because there was no way that he could have his daughter wandering into Sunday service visibly fallen as I was.

I stumbled out of the house on numb feet, trembling.

And the men in suits were there.

They opened the door to the limousine and bade me to get inside. I obeyed, because I had reverted to being obedient again, there at the center of my grand demolition.

"What does the paperwork demand of me?" I asked.

The men looked at me, hard, neither of them sympathetic at all. "You must stay away from here for a period of five years at least. You must never attempt to contact Prince Hercules. You must never come to the country. If you do that, the sum of money will be yours."

He pointed to a figure outlined on the contract, and my vision blurred. I would never have to work again. My child would want for nothing. And given that I was currently homeless, that was important.

But I could only think of one thing.

"How many times have you had to do this for him?"

"All these things are a matter of private palace business. Will you sign or not?"

And I knew that I'd been had. My virginity taken by a careless seducer of women. He hadn't waited for me because he cared; he had simply waited until it was legal. And then he had sent strangers to do this to me. To dehumanize me, to take what had been a beautiful gift on my part and turn it into something tawdry and worse than common.

"I'll sign."

And so I had. Because what other choice did I have?

Yes, I remembered the first time I saw Hercules Xenakis.

It had been the beginning of the utter destruction of my life as I knew it.

But I rebuilt it into something beautiful. Something that centered around our daughter. *My* daughter.

And I did not violate that agreement. Not in that whole time. Except...

Except I had come back to Medland for the first time, at the end of my five-year exile. And there had been rumors he would be here in the lead-up to his wedding.

I'd told myself I was going for a walk.

But that walk ended at a place I knew I was likely to find him.

There he was on a balcony at the country club, overlooking the ocean below. With a woman standing next to him, a giant ring glittering on her fourth finger. I knew who she was—I wasn't a fool. I didn't avoid headlines about him. I didn't seek them out either. I refused to let him become a sickness for me, ever again.

But I knew he was getting married.

A part of me had to wonder if I was here out of a true desire to reconcile with my mother, now that my father was gone, or if I had really come in the hope of this.

Because of course he still came here. This site of my ruin. The site of his betrayal.

And he was with her.

There had been many *hers* over the years.

I'd forced myself to look at them all and imagine what lies he told them.

But seeing them in person...

It made my whole body ache. I suddenly wished that I had Lily with me. Because at least then I could've turned to her, used her as some sort of distraction.

No.

I would never, ever allow Lily to be exposed to him.

He didn't want her. He didn't want her, and he didn't deserve to see her. Did not deserve to set eyes on the miracle that we had created. The only good and beautiful thing that I had in my life. He had rejected her, and he never, ever deserved to have even a moment of that pure love that she possessed.

But then he turned, as if an invisible force had tapped him on the shoulder. And his eyes caught mine.

And the expression I saw there was one of pure hatred.

CHAPTER TWO

Hercules

MARISSA. HER NAME echoed inside me, as it always had. And for one moment I was stopped utterly and completely. For one moment I was transported back in time. To the strangest, most unaccountable three years of my life.

Three summers spent obsessed with a dowdy brunette who hadn't even known who I was upon our first meeting.

That was what had intrigued me at first. Women tried all kinds of things to get close to me. To get into my sphere and seize whatever power they thought they might have. But not her.

Oh, I hadn't believed her doe-eyed innocence at first. I had been waiting for her to show her hand at some point, the whole summer that first time we met. But there was never a hand to show.

We never exchanged names, and if she knew that I was Hercules Xenakis, Prince of Pelion, she did not let on.

I talked to her. And I could not remember a time

when I had ever talked to another person the way that I did her. And even now, years later, I could not quite account for why.

At first, it had felt like a game. I was one of the most recognizable men in the world and had been from the day of my birth, so the novelty of being anonymous was one that amused me greatly.

But there came a point where I began avoiding any and all others on Sunday afternoons so that I could go and meet the pastor's daughter, who had somehow captured my attention.

She became a sickness.

I was obsessed with her smile. Her eyes. The way the sunlight caught her hair and created a halo of gold around her. Like she was an angel. The kind who shouldn't associate with a devil like me.

It has never been my habit to question my motivations. An entire staff of hundreds exists, and always has, to see to my every whim. I've never had to put much thought into why I do anything. If I want something, it appears.

And so I didn't put any thought into why my little fascination had a hold of me the way that she did. It was innocent, that first summer.

But things changed.

The way that she looked at me, with that hunger in her eyes. And I knew that she didn't understand what was burning between us, which should have been my first warning to stay away.

But as the Prince of Pelion, I did not have to heed warnings. The world rearranged itself around my desires, so denying myself the diversion never crossed my mind.

My first mistake, and one that I would come to un-derstand as a weakness.

The kind of weakness that my father worked to train out of me from the time I was a boy.

A man, in my father's opinion, had to be able to with-stand anything. Any pain, any betrayal, without a hint of emotion. If his child was to be tortured in order for an enemy to gain secrets, the man must not bend then.

He had done his best to ensure that I could withstand any physical torture.

Even if he'd had to be the one to test me.

And he had.

But in my father's view of the world, that same man could not put shackles on his excess. It was balance, he had told me, that a man be the hardest, cruelest of weapons when the time came, and that he indulged his baser urges when it was not a time of war.

Well-fed appetites for drink and women contributed to strength in lean times, or so he'd said.

Weakness in himself was the only thing that a ruler need fear. My father ruled Pelion with an iron fist, and he ruled his life the same way.

He ruled his children in that manner as well. Mak-ing sure that from infancy I was fit to take the throne when he passed on. If he could have taken on the Roman practice of leaving his issue out in the dirt overnight to see if it was strong enough to survive, I knew he would have done so.

Being the son of King Xerxes was not for the faint of heart. Or mind or body.

But one petite brunette that I met on the shores of a deserted ocean could hardly be a threat. That was what I told myself.

My heart had been forged in fire, covered in iron from the time I was a child. I excelled at playing a part. The international playboy who cared for nothing.

But in truth, behind the scenes, I was always ensuring that my father did no damage to the country. Did no damage to my mother.

For her part, she removed herself from the palace whenever she could.

I had been hurt by that, as a boy. Left to my father's particular brand of care, which included torture and time spent in solitary confinement.

I'd ached for my mother then.

But there was no point in regretting anything.

My father had made me a weapon. One intent on being turned around on him.

And I would have engaged in a more open rebellion in the beginning if I had not known it would come back tenfold on my much younger sister and the Queen.

There was no place in my life for softness, nor any place for a commoner who would endanger the plans that I had carefully put in place.

The Council of Pelion and I worked together to find an existing precedent for change of leadership. Once the current ruler surpassed his seventieth birthday, if the successor had produced an heir, he could take control.

It was a complicated process, and as I did not want to create a Civil War, I knew I had to play my cards right.

My father was nothing if not a self-preservationist. And I knew that I would have to do everything in my power to have the full favor of the people. And that meant, of course, marrying a woman from Pelion, one who came from the high echelons of society and who was well loved by many.

And I had done my part. I had managed to gain an agreement from my father that he would allow this, once his birthday passed and I had fulfilled my obligations.

One of which was marrying a woman he found suitable.

But in my foolishness, I had begun to negotiate in my own mind, as one summer with Marissa turned to two. And then it became three, and the heat of passion had burned between us, so hot and bright it obliterated the memory of any woman who had come before her.

I had to leave, had to return to Pelion to make a case for why this woman was worth upending the existing agreement that I had with the daughter of a politician.

But when I returned to Medland she was gone. Nowhere to be found at all. Her father simply opened the door with a stony face and said she had gone.

And I wondered if she had gone off on the mission trip she had spoken of all that time ago, but it had seemed to me that her devotion had rather turned to the worship of me and my body rather than a deity.

I was not content with that. I sent my security detail out on a search for her, engaged the resources of the palace, and still, it turned up nothing.

She had abandoned me.

The woman that I had been willing to risk an agreement over was gone.

No one had ever dared to defy me before.

That she would felt like a near unendurable blow, one that had left a great crack inside my chest.

But I had repaired that. Let it go.

Still, as I stood there, looking at her and her shocked face, I knew that it wasn't fully repaired. No. But it had changed.

It had been pain at first—a shock to me, as I had no idea I was capable of such fine feelings. But then it had changed, shifted into a deep, raging fury that had propelled me on. Had cemented my motives.

I had allowed myself to become distracted, and that was unacceptable.

I had gone back to Pelion, reaffirmed my commitment to my future marriage.

And now, five years on, it was set to take place. It had all been put on hold until my fiancée, Vanessa, was ready, and I had been happy enough to wait, as I knew that I could not rush something like this, so poised on the knife's edge.

Once, once I had been impatient. Once I had nearly ruined everything. It would not happen again.

Except, I forgot why in the moment that I stared at Marissa.

But there came a point where I began avoiding any and all others. And then she did what she had done that first day, the very first time I saw her.

She turned and she ran away.

I spared a glance at the woman by my side. "I have business to attend to."

"What is it?" she asked, only half-interested.

She was more interested in taking in the surroundings at the country club's deck. And the people who were there. Not so she could see them so much as she could know who had seen her. Vanessa was accustomed to status and luxury. It was one thing I valued in her.

Vanessa and I had an arrangement that centered squarely on politics and personal gain. She was not interested in my comings and goings, not any more than I was interested in hers.

She tucked her blond hair behind her ear, and her ring glittered in the light. "If I don't return soon, have security detail escort you back to the house."

"Very thoughtful of you," she responded, smiling at me, ever conscious of the fact that we might be photographed at a given moment.

A good thing she remembered, because I could not spare a thought for it. I charged away from the deck, going back the way that Marissa had gone. And I saw just enough to see which direction she fled, rounding a corner down one of the quaint streets.

I wondered if she was going to her parents' house, though I had checked periodically for months with palace security, and they swore she had not gone to her parents' home.

But she was here, so clearly something had changed.

It occurred to me suddenly that I should perhaps feel like a fool, chasing down the footsteps of a ghost from my past wearing a custom-made suit on the night of my engagement party. But I was a man who was accustomed to his word being law, and the matter felt as if it bore more importance than it did.

So I felt it. So it was.

And I ignored the slight kick in my gut that told

me it was a shade too close to something my father might think.

I didn't know why I was going after her. I'd had countless lovers before her, and countless sins stained my soul.

I didn't know why she mattered.

Because she got beneath the armor. That was why. Because she had done something to me that no one else had ever done. Not before, not since. Because she had made me question my primary goal in life. Had made me question the very foundation that it had been built upon.

Because of her, I nearly put the plan to rescue my nation in jeopardy.

I would have chanced marrying a commoner, a woman unapproved, who could add nothing to the throne, ensuring that my father stayed seated for years longer than he might have otherwise.

My father was too mean to die. Far too cruel to do anything quite so prosaic as give up the ghost.

And she had walked away from me. It was not I who had come to my good senses, no.

It both incensed and fascinated me even still, and that was why—I told myself—I was now chasing after her through the streets of Medland.

Her family home was small, a classic saltbox house with shingled siding like every other house on the street. I crossed the lawn, prepared to walk in without knocking, because princes did not knock, when I realized that it was probably for the best if I attempted to open with a small modicum of courtesy, as I had no idea if her parents still lived there, or if it was the home she had in fact gone into.

I rapped on the door and waited.

It opened wide, to reveal an older woman with the same color eyes as Marissa. She swung the door just wide enough that I caught sight of Marissa standing behind her. Marissa quickly retreated into the kitchen. The older woman looked behind her. "Can I help you?"

"I think we both know why I'm here."

"I don't, I'm afraid. I'm the only one here."

I admired how brazen she was. But that didn't mean that I was going to allow her to get away with it.

"I'm here for your daughter."

"She is not here for you," the woman said. "How dare you show your face?"

No one save my father had ever spoken to me with that tone of voice. This woman, who only came to the middle of my chest, spoke as if she would cheerfully remove my head from my shoulders. "Go off and have your wedding. Leave us in peace."

"I have questions for Marissa."

"And she has none for you. If she did, she would be out here. My daughter is strong. Made stronger because of you. We don't need you here."

"I am very sorry," I said, feeling nothing of the kind. "But I can't take no for an answer."

I stepped inside, and she moved back, allowing the entry. My footsteps fell heavy on the wood floor, and I knew that was what signaled Marissa, who came charging in from the next room.

Damn, she was beautiful.

Even more than the last time I'd seen her. She'd been

a woman then, but she… She had blossomed in the years since.

Her curves were more exaggerated, hollows in her cheekbones, rather than the pleasant roundness that had been there before. Her dark hair was long, curling at the ends, and there was a wildness to it now. I had thought, the first time I'd seen her, that she did look every inch the church secretary.

She did not now.

There was an edge of sophistication to the way she was dressed, even though it was simple and not designed to draw attention to her. She was wearing makeup, which I had never known her to do before.

I resented it. I wanted to wipe it away, just like I wanted to wipe away the years. Wanted to go back to a time when things had made sense to me in a way that they never had before.

When my world had been contained in an empty stretch of shore and this woman.

But I had been wrong then. Wrong about what mattered. Wrong about everything. So there was no point going back.

And there was no point mourning the passing of the years.

"How dare you?" she asked. "My mother told you to leave."

"And I said no." I took a step forward. "Have you forgotten who I am, Marissa?"

"In the five years since I've seen you? Almost. Your name has not crossed my lips once, Hercules. This is the first time in all that time. I swear it."

Her expression was guarded, the words hard, and

she was nothing like the girl I had once known. And I believed her.

"I want to know where you went."

"You want to know where I went?" Confusion and anger contorted her beautiful features.

And it hit me then that however much Marissa had changed, it was strange that she was angry at me.

She was the one who had left. And I had racked my brain over the years to try to think of reasons why. But I had been faithful to her. And yes, I had gone back to Pelion and left her in Medland, but I had assumed she would understand I would be back. And I had been.

She was the one who had abandoned us. A good thing, I could see now. But that made me question why rage still burned in my chest.

I heard the clatter of footsteps on the stairs, but they did not sound heavy or even enough to be an adult's. I looked and saw a little girl leaping down the steep staircase, her dark curls bouncing with the motion. And everything in me went still. I'm not a man who believes in premonitions. I believe in what can be seen, felt and touched, but in that moment, I felt something supernatural steal over me.

And when that child looked up at me, her chocolate eyes connecting with mine, I felt a stirring of recognition down in my soul.

I knew this girl. I, who had never had exposure to any child and who had never had a strong feeling about one, was suddenly overcome, immobilized by the strength of the connection that I felt to this one.

Because looking in her eyes was like looking into a mirror. I recognized her face, because it was mine, but smaller, rounder, cherubic in a way I was certain I had never been. I looked up at Marissa and saw she had gone pale.

"What the hell game are you playing?"

CHAPTER THREE

Marissa

IT WAS THE shock on his face that confused me. I don't know what I had been prepared for. But I had always rejected the idea that he might lay eyes on Lily, because he didn't deserve to. Because he had rejected her. I had thought in terms of protecting my daughter, because what mother wouldn't? He didn't deserve to see what a wonderful child we created, because he had rejected her. Because he had sold her when he bought my silence.

But the look on his face was not that of a man who saw this child as being inconsequential. No. The look that he had on his face was that of a man who was… shocked. As though he had been struck by lightning. Of all the things I had expected, I had not expected this. I had done my best never to think about it, of course. But…

No, something was wrong about the way he was looking at her, and I knew it. Deep down I knew. I had seen his face when he thought no one was looking. That sort of blank hardness that I'd witnessed on his features the first day I'd seen him all those years ago.

I'd seen him smile. Laugh.

I'd watched as his guard dropped completely and he'd given himself over to pleasure.

But I had never seen him look like this.

It was not rage; it was something beyond that. His skin had taken on a waxen pallor, and for the first time he seemed...

Well, human, and not so like a god.

"Explain this," he said, his voice hard.

My mother looked at him and then at me, her expression helpless.

My mother had worked hard to repair the relationship that had been severed by my father. She had secretly traveled to visit me and Lily a few times over the years. And I hated that my father's death had brought me a sense of relief, but it had. Because it had returned my childhood home to me, and my mother and I no longer had to stoop to subterfuge to see one another.

She felt nothing but sympathy for me, and I wondered if sometimes she felt a bit of envy.

Because I'd found a sort of passion that had made me behave the way that I had.

Because I had then gone out and raised a child on my own, which she'd not had the courage to do.

In spite of how unhappy she had been.

And now I could see that she was prepared to fight for Lily and me if need be.

"What do you mean what is this?" I asked. "You know perfectly well."

"I don't know anything," he said, his eyes never leaving Lily.

"We cannot have this conversation in front of her," I said.

Lily, being four and full of inquisitiveness without an ounce of perception, tilted her head back and stared up at the man I knew to be her father.

"Who are you?" she asked him.

"I was going to ask you the same thing," he responded, his voice far too hard to speak to a child.

"I'm Lily Rivero," she said. "It's nice to meet you."

Lily was precocious and polite, and I was happy that I had been able to stay home and take care of her. That we'd been able to afford to buy a wonderful house in a beautiful neighborhood. I had made the absolute most of all that I had been given, if for no other reason than to throw it in the face of Hercules, whether he could see it or not.

When he looked at me, the fury in his eyes was terrifying. It wasn't fire. It was like ice. And I sensed that it had the power to utterly destroy me.

But then, he always had. He was my weakness. My undoing.

My brightest and most beautiful sin.

My father had repeated the quote that the wages of sin was death.

Looking at Hercules now, I was beginning to wonder.

The words were quite literal and not spiritual as I had originally taken them to mean.

"Perhaps there is a place where we can talk," he said.

And I feared slightly for my own safety and health. It was like staring at a stranger. A large, incredibly muscular stranger, who bore no small amount of anger inside him.

But then…

The light hit him, just so, a shaft of sun coming through the window. And I knew him.

It was like being cast back to those sunny days on the beach.

When I had trusted him. When I had given myself to him.

When I had known him, better than I had ever known anyone.

It was still true.

That this man would always have a piece of me that no one else would. What we had shared, my father had called a *sin*. The result of which he had called the *consequence*.

But it had been *intimacy*.

And it had been real.

Whatever had happened after, it had been real for me.

And that was why I found myself unable to deny him. That was why, in spite of the years of pain, anger and anguish, I could not deny this man now when he asked for an audience with me.

Or maybe I was weak.

I would have to allow for that, I knew. I had always been weak for Hercules.

But strong for Lily.

Strong for Lily from the very beginning.

I would be strong for her now.

I followed him into the kitchen, and then I gestured to the back door. It was his turn to follow me, out to the backyard with a scant covering of crabgrass, peppered down a rolling slope.

You could just barely see the ocean through the trees,

the most beautiful views on the island not afforded to a family like mine.

I had always found that unfair when I was a child. That the bright, brilliant ocean views were granted to those who only lived here a few months out of the year.

As an adult, of course, I understood. The cost of such beauty.

I looked back at Hercules, and my previous thought echoed in my head.

The cost of such beauty.

I knew the cost of touching beauty like his.

Or so I'd thought.

I had not realized a further payment might be required.

"Is she mine?" The question was a growl.

It took me a full minute to process those words. Because it was not the question I had expected him to ask.

There had been papers. Demands. He had never wanted her. He didn't want me.

"How can you ask me that?" I sputtered.

"What else could I ask? Is that child mine?"

"You know she is," I said. "You know. You sent men. You made me sign papers. I was never supposed to come and see you, and here you are at my parents' house…"

"What men? What papers?"

"They were your men," I said. "Men from the palace. I called, Hercules. So many times. I was pregnant, and I was terrified. And do you have any idea what my father…? I needed you. I needed you, and you sent a nondisclosure agreement."

"I did no such thing," he said.

The light in his eyes had gone obsidian, and for the first time I was staring full in the face of the blackness I had witnessed in that unguarded moment when he thought no one had been looking at him that first day I'd seen him.

There was something beneath that careless playboy facade that the paper saw, something beneath the caring lover that I had spent time with years ago.

It was something I had not touched. Had not tasted. Until now.

"I don't know what to tell you," I said. "I called the palace and left messages, and no one returned them. Finally, I said… I told them that I was pregnant with your baby."

"You told someone at the palace?"

"Yes. There was nothing else I could do."

"You told someone at the palace and then men arrived." It wasn't a question, more grim statement.

"Yes. Men came, and they offered me a sum of money if I never spoke to you again. If I never contacted you again."

"You took a payoff in order to avoid telling me about my child?"

"I thought you were the one offering the payoff," I said, my heart fluttering in my chest like a trapped bird. I was beginning to feel sick, because the implications of the words being spoken between us were starting to turn over inside of me, revealing facets that I had not immediately understood or seen. "I didn't choose money over you. I thought you were demanding that I never see you…"

"This child is my heir," he said.

"She's a girl," I said, defensively.

"That doesn't matter. A law as old as time in my country, which my father would have changed if he could have, believe me. But he could not, alas for him. And so it remains. Any child of mine—as long as she is legitimate—can take the throne."

"Well," I said, drawing myself up as tall as I possibly could. I still fell laughably short of the top of his shoulder. "She's not legitimate. She won't be. She can't be. Surely you know that already."

"That isn't how it works. If I choose to recognize her by marrying you, then she will be legitimate."

"I don't... I don't understand any of this," I said, panic rising up inside of me.

How was I supposed to make sense of it? I had thought all these years that he never wanted to see her. That he would rather pay exorbitant sums to keep Lily and myself as his dirty secret. Making sense of the fact that he seemed to want Lily was almost impossible.

It was untangling a web that had been stretched across my life five years ago. One that I had built myself with the remnants I'd had left.

I'd lost him.

I'd lost my parents.

And now here he was, larger than life and every inch as heartbreakingly beautiful as he'd been at the first, and he was telling me that he wanted Lily.

"This is my father's doing," he said, reiterating what he'd said before. "He and I have an agreement. I don't know if you know much about the history of my country."

"I steer clear of everything concerning you to the best of my ability."

His lip lifted into a curl. "Except for my money."

Anger sizzled through my veins. "I'm sorry. Should I have sat in poverty and virtue with your child after being rejected by you and by my parents? Would that have made a more beautiful and sympathetic picture of maternal suffering for you? When I had an offer of comfort and riches on the table, should I have opted to take something else? There is no shame in poverty, not when life has given you no choice. But I was given a choice. A choice to make sure that no matter what happened, my child would have food. Would have shelter. That I would be able to be home to take care of her. I have been all she's had. Her only parent. It is my job, and mine alone, to care for her. There has been no one else. If you would have preferred to come back to a life in ruin so that you could rebuild it again, I am sorry to disappoint you. When you left, my life *was* ruin. My father looked at me and called me a whore. I had nowhere and nothing, and I rebuilt it with what I was given. I will not feel shame for that."

"Do you know what I think?"

I crossed my arms and took a step toward him, and I could see shock flickered behind his dark eyes. If he thought that I was still the young girl in love that he had met back then, then he was to be reeducated, and quickly.

Five years I had been without him. Five years I had been on my own in the world. Learning what it meant to live beneath the judgment of others, sleepless nights spent caring for my daughter, without any help when I found myself in a state of utter exhaustion.

And I had become strong.

Arguments in doctors' offices when I knew my child had pneumonia and they simply wanted to send me home. Standing up for Lily when she had pushed someone to the ground in her preschool class because they had said her mother was bad since Lily didn't have a father.

Standing up for myself when people sometimes didn't let their children associate with mine for those same reasons.

Years alone and motherhood had sharpened me, and sometimes I resented it.

Because I had been soft once, and I had believed in love.

The only kind of love left that I believed in was the kind between a mother and daughter, strengthened when my own had attempted to mend the bridge that had been broken between us by my father.

Fathers I could do without, thank you.

Mothers I had found strength in.

But like a stone battered about, my smooth edges had been cracked against the hardships of life, creating hard, sharp edges.

And he was about to understand just how much I'd changed.

"I'm sure you're going to tell me what you think," I said, "because you think the world stops and starts on your word. Because once you were able to make my world stop and start at your word. But I made a life without you in it. And I will tell you gladly that there is nothing for you here. So whatever you say, it better be compelling, and not predictable as I suspect it will be."

"I think that you didn't want to hassle with me, and when you were offered a payoff, you took it rather than making sure you did the right thing."

I scoffed. "The right thing? The right thing. To ensure that a man who goes about the world spreading his seed whenever he feels the urge knows about a child he didn't even want? How many other women are like me, do you think?"

He drew back. "None."

"You don't know that."

"I have always used condoms," he said ferociously. "With every other woman."

"Oh," I said. "So I'm special. The woman who had never even touched a man's hand before you is the one that you couldn't be bothered to protect? I'm glad that our dalliance meant so much to you."

"Say what you want, Marissa, but I came back for you. I came back for you, and you were not here. And a damn good thing, I have told myself over the years, because I had a responsibility to my country and to my people, and you did not fit anywhere into that responsibility. But now there is her. Lily. And I cannot ignore the implications of her existence. My father has ruled Pelion with an iron fist for generations. And the only reason that I have not overthrown him in some kind of civil war is that the casualties would be too great, and there is a law that states the current leader is to step aside at seventy if the successor has married and produces an heir. I found that suitable woman some time ago."

"Yes. I know. I've seen photos of you with her."

"But Lily is my heir. And my father has had a significant birthday. That ushers in a new order in my country immediately. And that must be fulfilled. Because over the years my father's tyrannical tendencies have gotten worse. He is beginning to crack down on even the most basic of freedoms people in my country used to experience. And while there is breath in my body and power to do so, I cannot allow it. But the consideration of the cost to civilian life and the danger to my mother and sister has weighed heavily on me. But this… We have a binding document."

"Your father is a tyrant—do you think he would honor it?"

"It is not him that I need to honor it. It is the military. They serve the King. Not only that, it's whether or not I am King in the eyes of allies."

"It all seems trivial to me."

"It is the nature of being royal. Tradition is what it is."

"But will I be deemed acceptable?"

"That is for the Council to decide, but I suspect that the existence of an heir and the law as it is written will trump any concerns about your suitability."

"I have a life. I have built a life for Lily and myself in Boston. I am terribly sorry about your country. Not for your sake, but for the sake of your people.But I fail to see how it's my problem."

"It is your problem because you had my child."

I stepped forward, rage simmering in my blood, boiling over. "She is my child. Your contribution to her genetics does not make you a father. It does not make her yours. I gave birth alone. The pain and fear that I felt in that moment was horrible, and if not for a nurse who felt sorry for me and sat there and held my hand the entire time, there would've been no one there for me. I took an infant back to my home by myself, and I'm the one who didn't sleep for months. I'm the one who paced the halls rocking a crying baby."

I took a jagged breath and continued, all my anger— at him, my parents, the world—spilling out now. "And you… You were at parties. You had a new lover that same week that I gave birth, and she was on the cover of magazines with you, all slim and beautiful and per- fectly made up, and my hair was in one giant mat, my pajama pants were too tight and I wanted to weep from lack of sleep. Lily is *mine*. She is mine by rights. You have parties. And endless photos to document the way that you enjoy spending your time, and all the glitter- ing, sparkling objects you can lay claim to. But I am not one of them, and neither is she. Your father might be a bastard, but it's his money that kept us off the streets, if I'm understanding this correctly."

His face went grim, the light behind his eyes un- readable, opaque.

"I don't have room for emotion in this," he said. "There is a means here to liberate my country, and it will be done. Lily is coming with me whether or not you like it."

"What are you going to do?"

"Take her from you forcibly if I must, and deal with whatever fallout results. But I would rather that you came with me, as it would make things easier for the child."

Horror stole through me, and I could see that he

wasn't kidding. I could see the hardness in him. And I wondered how in the world I had ever thought this man to be a creature of pleasure and lightness, when I could see now that he was all rock and cold.

"You can't do this."

"I can. Even legally. I have diplomatic immunity, first of all. Second of all, Lily is a citizen of Pelion. And I am her father."

"Your name isn't on the birth certificate."

"It doesn't matter. Or have you not been listening? I am a prince in line to be a king and my word is law, even here."

I felt some of the fight begin to drain out of me, but then I steeled myself, took a breath and did my best to renew it. "I will not go easily. I will not uproot my child from everything that she knows, everything that she is, because you have decided that it's time to take responsibility."

"I didn't know. And if you want to make it about Lily, then you have to ask yourself what the ramifications of your decision are. She could be Queen."

The words shocked me, because it had honestly never occurred to me. That Lily was royal. That she was a princess. One that was in line for the throne of Pelion, but only if Hercules and I married.

"Would you rob your child of her rightful place in this world?"

I didn't want my child to be a queen. That was my very first thought. Because the very idea of her being a world leader, of her having such scrutiny placed on her, such a broad target painted on her back... It filled me with dread. I couldn't stand it when children made fun

of her parentage. The very idea of her being a leader—
a woman leader in this world—and the kinds of things
that would be said about her… It scared me to my bones.

But on the other hand, there was a truth to what he
said that I found difficult to deny.

But the idea of being married to this man that I had
hated for so long, who had hurt me so much…

A little bubble welled up inside my chest, and I despised it. Because I recognized it for what it was.

Joy.

That I could feel joy in some part of myself that
Hercules was back, that he was proposing marriage…

Well, it made me feel like the foolish idiot my father thought I was. The immoral fool who would throw
over all scruples and morality for the touch of a good-
looking man.

This wasn't about me. And if I was to claim truth for
all the things that I'd said to him in the past few minutes, I had to take myself out of the equation.

I had to think of Lily. Only of Lily.

"It's not my permission you need," I said. "But you
will ask my daughter's."

"I'm sorry," he responded, arching a black brow.
"You expect me to go to a child and explain all of this."

"She has friends," I said. "She's just now reconnect-
ing with her grandmother. It is her future you're talking
about, and yes, I know she's four. And I know that…" I
blinked back tears, because I knew that what my daughter would see was this tall, beautiful man telling her that
he was her father. And that she was a princess. And I
already knew what Lily would say.

But it was that vision in my mind that made me so resolute.

That Lily would be a princess. That she would have a father.

Whatever my feelings about him were...

He hadn't known.

He hadn't rejected me. He hadn't rejected her. And I couldn't shrug off the layers of armor that I had put on over the years with the ease of that revelation, but it was what made me give him time to speak, rather than simply attempting to run him through with a kebab skewer that I might have found in my mother's kitchen drawer.

"It's her life," I said. "And so, yes. I expect you to speak to her." I sighed heavily. "If she says no...you'll have to kidnap us both, I guess."

CHAPTER FOUR

Hercules

UTTER DISBELIEF FIRED through me as I stared down at Marissa. I hardly recognized the woman who stood before me, and I had known her intimately five years ago. But she was not the scared creature who had fled, no matter that I had thought she might be, given the way she had run from me back at the restaurant.

She had not been running to protect herself, but to protect Lily.

Lily.

Who was undeniably mine.

But I could not afford to falter, could not afford to allow emotion to have any purchase on this moment, because I had a responsibility.

First and foremost, Lily was the heir to the throne of Pelion. Lily was the key to ousting my father from power, and she would have to be treated as such.

But somehow I had been thrust into a position where I was going to have to make political negotiations with a child.

Marissa was staring me down, her dark eyes never

wavering from mine, and I had no doubt that everything she said was true.

I would have to bundle them up and carry them out of
the house, forcing them onto a plane, if I did not do this.

Now, whatever Marissa thought, I was not ashamed
at the thought that I might take that action. I would do
what I had to do.

But I was also happy to avoid it, given it was an action that was guaranteed to draw press.

It was a tangled mess. I was set to marry Vanessa in
just two weeks' time, and now there was no question
of that happening.

I didn't need allegations of me being a kidnapper to
come out on top of it.

I was not a man who dealt in uncertainty—a man
in my position could not afford to be. But as I followed
Marissa up the stairs, I felt a shadow of it. And I realized that the only reason I even knew what I could be
feeling was because of her. Because Marissa had, all
those years ago, taken that bedrock certainty of who I
was—and my confidence that I could make whatever
life I chose to arrange for myself—and dashed it against
the rocks, as if she were the siren to my wayward sailor.

She pushed the door open at the top of the stairs, and
I followed her in. "Lily," she said, "Hercules would like
to speak to you." There was a tremor in her voice for the
first time. And if I had been a different man, I might
have felt some uncertainty along with it.

But I could not afford to waver. Not ever. And I could
not afford sympathy in any measure.

Lily looked confused. Curious. Her dark eyes swept
over me, and even amid the confusion, even in her

youth, I could see an imperiousness there. Inherited, I knew.

Lily.

What would her name have been if I had been there? Her name would have been a family name. Aphrodite or Apollonia, perhaps.

Lily was so simple.

It sounded like something that could be easily crushed, and everything inside of me rebelled at that. But when I looked back down at the child and her steady expression as she looked me full in the face with an ease that men found next to impossible at times, I knew the name suited her well.

Because her enemies would never know that she was made of steel at her core. They would be distracted and confused by her apparent softness, and they would never see her hit coming.

I would teach her to hone that. I would teach her all she needed in order to ascend the throne of Pelion. She was young enough that it was not too late, and I might have missed her earliest years, but I would not miss anymore. I kept my gaze on Lily, because this discussion was between us, and only us.

"I have something I wish to speak to you about," I said, trying to decide if I should loom over the child or crouch down and meet her eyes.

I was a prince. I did not crouch. It was near to a bow, and I wasn't entirely sure my body could form such a submissive posture.

But speaking over her as I was didn't seem right either.

And so for the first time I could remember, I bent a knee.

"Your mother and I were…" How the hell did you explain such a thing to a child? I had no idea. Did she even know a man and woman had to *know* each other in order to reproduce? And I could not say something that would cast her mother in a negative light. That was just diplomacy. She was on her mother's side. Clearly, she would not take kindly to an interloper telling her that her mother was anything less than perfect. So I would have to select my wording carefully. Not out of deference to Marissa, but out of care for my particular political mission.

With a four-year-old.

My child. My *daughter*.

It was something I could not fathom still. It settled on my skin like a crackle of electricity, rather than sinking in.

"We knew each other for a time," I continued. "And we were…separated. I had to go back to my country, and you moved away from here."

She scrunched up her face. "You talk funny. Is it because you're from another country?"

It was not a question I expected, and one that came in slightly from left field, given the direction my line of speaking was headed.

"Yes," I said. "I imagine so." Though, I did not think I had a very marked accent. I've been told my English was nothing short of excellent.

"Okay," she said, apparently satisfied by my admission.

"I am from a country far away," I continued. "Across

the ocean. An island in the middle of the Mediterranean Sea. It's beautiful. You see, I had to return there to see to business because I am a prince."

"A prince?" Her eyes got round.

"Yes," I said, satisfied that that statement had landed anyway. "And I have just discovered something, Lily. You are my Princess. You're my daughter. I… I'm your father."

And then she did something I couldn't have anticipated.

I didn't realize that children felt emotion in that way, but she demonstrated to me that I knew nothing. Her face crumpled, almost immediately, and the sound that came out of her tiny body was almost inhuman. A high-pitched wail that pierced my heart, pierced any defense I thought I might have had. And then she wrapped her arms around my neck and held me, as if I weren't a stranger. As if I weren't a man who had stormed into her grandmother's house and made all manner of threats to her mother.

I went stiff, completely uncertain of what to do. And for the first time, I looked to Marissa. Her expression was neutral, but there were tears in her eyes. I tried to straighten, but Lily would not let me go. So I wrapped an arm around her and stood, holding her against me as she wept. "Your mother told me that I had to ask you," I continued, "if you want to come with your mother and live with me in my castle."

I realized how truly unfair a line of questioning that was, and also realized that by asking me to go and speak to Lily, Marissa had not set me up for failure. Her motive had not been selfish, not at all. Because anyone would know that a four-year-old would not have the willpower to turn down such an offer.

She lifted her head, wiping at her eyes with closed fists. "What about my nana?"

"Your nana can come too," I said. "It's a very big castle."

I didn't know how I'd come into the position of negotiating details of something so delicate with a preschooler, but there I was.

"Mommy," Lily said, her voice plaintive. She reached for Marissa.

Marissa stepped forward, and I transferred the warm weight of the child to her.

It was a strange thing, one that I imagined normal parents did.

Mine certainly never had. There had been no affection spared for me in my youth. I imagine my mother had felt inclined to give it to me, but my father had not allowed it.

And I...

I had spent so much time planning for what it would be like politically when I had an heir that I had never once spared a thought to what kind of father I would be.

Only what kind of king I might be.

But Lily was not a hypothetical—she was very real, and seemed to need something from me that I could not quite fathom, but knew I had to find it in myself to give.

"It's true," Marissa said, brushing Lily's hair back from her face. "Everything he said is true. You're a princess. If you want to be a princess, it means moving away from here. Away from our home in Boston. Away from what we know. But I'll be with you. And...

you were born a princess, Lily." Her voice broke. "You were born a princess, and whether you go to Pelion or not, you're still a princess. But everything that your father has belongs to you too. And it wouldn't be right for me to ask you not to have it."

It was clear to me that Lily didn't understand Marissa's impassioned speech. But I did. I appreciated how difficult this was for her, even though it couldn't affect my ultimate action.

Lily's expression was serious, and she looked at me with luminous eyes. "Daddy?"

The word hit like a bullet. I felt as though it had ripped its way through my chest and torn my heart utterly into pieces.

The heart that I didn't realize had been quite so vulnerable, or quite so...

Quite so able to feel.

This child was innocent. Of everything.

Of what had happened between her mother and me, whether it was subterfuge on the part of Marissa or not. Of the royal lineage she had been born into.

She had no control over any of it, and I knew exactly what that felt like.

Except when my father had taken me in hand, they had been the hands of a monster, and there had never been any question that I call him something so affectionate as Daddy.

But this child was handing me trust. A moniker of affection that I had done nothing to earn, and I feared might never.

I felt utterly and wildly adrift in that moment, in a way that I had only ever done two other times in my life.

The first time I had seen Marissa—when it hadn't even been sexual in nature—and when I had come back to discover she was gone.

"Yes," I said, my voice less than steady, which was unacceptable.

And yet we were not in the throne room. Not before the press.

It was just me and this child. My child.

And Marissa.

"I want to go with you," the little girl said, while simultaneously tightening her hold on her mother.

"Then we will go together," Marissa said, holding even more tightly to Lily. "We will go together."

"And you will be my wife," I returned. "My Princess. Both of you."

I was resolved. And it was done.

"My mother?"

"Is welcome to come."

Marissa nodded slowly. "Okay. I'll... I'll talk to her."

"We must leave tonight," I said, decisively. "I will send men to handle my things, and to handle Vanessa as well."

"Oh..." Marissa looked crestfallen. "Vanessa. What are you going to do about Vanessa? You're engaged to her. You're supposed to get married in two weeks. How are you going to...?"

"I just told you," I replied. "I will send men to handle her. And to help mitigate any disappointment that she might feel. I'm not a monster. Whatever you might think."

"You're breaking up with your fiancée via your goon squad. Who, by the way, are likely the very same men who told me that you wanted—"

She cut herself off, and I saw her flick a glance at Lily.

"You and I will have to discuss this at another time."

"We will."

I picked up my phone. "Have my private jet ready to go in one hour. Please arrange alternative transport for Ms. Carlson."

And with that I hung up, not cowed by Marissa's disapproving gaze. She could disapprove all she wanted. We were in a mess that I suspected had been made by my father, and I refused to let him win. Absolutely and utterly refused. Marissa may not have liked my methods, but I knew that in the end my way would be the best way.

"An hour? That's not enough time to pack. What about all our things? Lily and I don't live here. We have a house in Boston. All of her toys…"

"Someone will be sent to retrieve them," I replied. "But I will not delay taking the two of you back to your rightful place."

"My mother…"

"I suggest you speak to her quickly."

"So all of this will be your way?" Marissa asked.

"I did this part your way," I said, nodding toward Lily, indicating the fact that I had asked her permission. "Yes. The rest will be done mine. I regret to tell you that there is no other option."

"Somehow, I very much doubt that you're filled with regret of any kind."

But she was wrong. Because what I felt swirling in my chest right now as I looked at my child, as I looked at the way she fitted in Marissa's arms, was a tangle of regret that I had not felt before in my entire life.

I did not like it. And so I did what I must do. I took action.

"We are going. Now. Don't tempt me to change the deadline."

Marissa turned away from me and bumped against a box on the edge of the dresser. She cursed—which surprised me—as the box hit the ground. The lid fell open and out spilled two shells. A larger one and a smaller one.

She looked at me, and my eyes went to her hair. The way it curled.

And then I looked back at the shells.

I'd given those to her. Because in my madness I'd seen her in everything, even in nature.

And she'd kept them. Even while claiming to hate me.

She bent down and picked up the box, put the shells back in and cradled the box to her chest. She stared me down for a moment, as if daring me to say something.

I didn't.

Then, without a word, Marissa nodded and swept from the room, leaving me standing there.

Something no one would typically dare to do.

But Marissa had never been typical. She hated me, and yet she had my shells. And I was fascinated all over again in spite of myself.

But Marissa had nothing to do with the decision that I had made.

This was about Lily. This was about the throne.

This was about making sure my father knew he would never win against me.

Of that I would be certain.

CHAPTER FIVE

Marissa

I HAD KNOWN that he was a prince. I had followed news stories about him over the years and seen the lavish way he lived his life in stunning photographs splashed across search engines and tabloid newspapers.

But it hadn't really taken hold of me just what that meant until we boarded his private plane.

Luxury on that scale was something so theoretical to me that I could only imagine it, and even then, I could only imagine it at a reduced scale.

My brain hadn't had the textural vocabulary for leather as soft as what was found on the plush couch in the seating area of the plane. It didn't have the concept of the scale that something like a prince's private plane might have. I had imagined something like I had seen in movies, where one still had to duck down when they stood, and there were a few seats with ample legroom, and glasses of champagne.

No.

This plane was mammoth. One that could easily fit the same number of people as commercial planes that did domestic flights. And there were rooms. Multiple rooms, though I didn't know what they all were.

The stewardess quickly ushered Lily to a beautifully appointed bedroom and did the same for my mother. Then she made herself vanish, and I knew that everyone had been carefully dealt with so that Hercules and I could talk.

My mother had of course decided to come with us. There was nothing left for her in Medland, except the beautiful house that she had once shared unhappily with my father.

I could tell that my mother was hesitant to leave me, but it was also clear to an extent that pushing back against Hercules was futile. Far better to try to negotiate with him and get a handle on what this new reality was. And what it would be in the future.

"This is…nice," I said, taking a seat on the couch and sinking into the buttery softness. But I refused to show him that I took pleasure in it.

"Champagne?" he asked.

"A toast to our upcoming union?" I asked. And I immediately regretted making the dry comment, because I was in no place where I could joke about such things.

I couldn't take it lightly.

It made my insides twist into a knot.

And that hope bubble in my chest became more pronounced.

I wanted to pop it.

I felt so foolish, revealing to him that I'd kept those shells. And even more foolish that I hadn't dumped them straight in the trash but had packed them instead.

"If you like."

"I don't drink," I said.

"Do you still not drink? I thought that you also didn't have premarital sex. And yet…"

I didn't tell him that I hadn't had sex since. That he was the only person I'd ever made the exception for.

I didn't tell him that I didn't drink because holdovers from my childhood were still hard to shake, and sometimes I worried a little bit about hellfire being in every breath I took wrong.

"Well, when do you suggest I might have started? During my pregnancy? After? When I was single parenting a young child? There never seemed a good time. And at the moments when I thought I might need a drink most, it occurred to me that perhaps it wasn't healthy to be thinking of it as a crutch."

"Fair enough."

He put the bottle of champagne back and then to my surprise opened a cooler and took out a bottle of sparkling cider.

"You can have champagne," I said.

"I don't need it," he said. "And, as you pointed out, perhaps if one is using it as a crutch, it's not a very good thing."

"I wouldn't think that Your Royal Highness needed crutches."

"In this current situation, I'm finding that I might need more than I think."

I didn't know what to say to that. The admission of weakness was so unexpected that it momentarily silenced me.

"Well, I find that I'm in want of some as well. But… but again, it seems an inadvisable reason to start."

"I don't disagree with you," he said. "And so, in the interest of fending off addictions, we can have this together."

"I did try to contact you," I said. "Whatever you think of me... I could have had much more if you would have known. Surely you must see that. If you can't believe in who I am as a person, if you can't believe that maybe what we had for a while was real, then believe that, even if I'm grasping, I'm not stupid. Believe that if I really wanted to take you for your money, I would have done so in a spectacular fashion. I would have shamed you publicly, but I had no interest in that. All I wanted was what was best for Lily. When those men came... Hercules, I thought I was nothing to you. Nothing more than one of the many women that you seduce and leave behind. I had no reason to believe that I was anything else. And I had no reason to believe those men were not sent by you."

He began to pour a glass of cider, and then he paused. Suddenly, the look on his face became one of stone. "It's why they couldn't find you," he said. "They didn't look. They were working for him, not for me. They had orders not to find you."

"What?"

"I searched for you," he said. "Your father said you were gone, and I didn't accept it. I had my men go after you. I had them search. I have resources that stretch far beyond that of a normal man. I should have been able to find you. They should have been able to find you. The fact that they did not..." He shook his head. "Why did I not realize it before now?"

"He wanted to keep you from her," I said.

"He did. Because he knew that when his birthday passed, I would succeed him. As is the law in Pelion. He wanted to delay my heir, wanted to set up hoops for me to jump through. Vanessa was a hoop. A suitable bride that was not ready to marry and reproduce immediately when my father passed his deadline."

"We don't need to punish each other," I said softly.

For the first time, I honestly felt some sympathy for him. He didn't know.

But I couldn't just turn my whole sense of the last five years on its head.

"I… I felt so utterly abandoned, Hercules. I betrayed who I thought I was for you."

He shook his head. "No. Don't tell me that. You are a strong woman, Marissa. If you did not want to have sex you wouldn't have."

The truth in those words set me back on my heels. He was right. I hadn't been seduced. Not in the way that I often let myself think of it. Yes, he was new and exciting, a window into sensations that I hadn't even known I wanted. But I had wanted him. I had wanted him deep in my soul. Wanted him with a desperation that defied sanity.

It reminded me of when he had asked me if I always did as I was told.

I had, because it had never occurred to me to do things a different way.

And when I stopped doing as I was told, it wasn't because I had simply replaced one set of commands with another.

It was because I had realized what I was. Who I was. And that I wanted it to be something different than I had been fashioned into.

It had nothing to do with faith, for mine had remained intact all these years. But it had become something deeper in many ways, something more personal, because I wasn't following commandments and dictates because my father said so, but because of what rang true in my own soul.

And perhaps I didn't have a life that looked perfect to everyone from the outside, but something in my heart felt healed.

No, it had never been about rebellion. It had never been about burning down what I believed in and starting from scratch.

It had been about finding me.

In the midst of everything that I had been taught to be, I found the person I was born to be.

I didn't have to hide. Not now. Not behind excuses, and not behind the idea that I had somehow succumbed to the temptation only because of his wickedness. Or even my own.

"It doesn't matter. Not now. I've changed. I assume you have too."

"No," he said, his expression opaque. "I have not changed. I am as I ever was. I'm a man who has the responsibility and the weight of an entire nation on his shoulders. And I never forget it. It doesn't matter what you see in the media. If you see photos of me looking carefree. All that time we spent together on the beach. I am never carefree."

I looked him right in the eyes. "I know that."

He appeared shocked by that. "What is it you think you know?"

"The first time that I saw you, standing there on the

shore. None of your friends had caught up to you yet, and you were standing there with your hands shoved into your pockets and a grim look on your face. You were clearly a man with a great weight on you. I could see it. A man who carried darkness around inside of him and understood that there might be a cost to that. I knew it. I did. I knew it then, and I know it now. All of what you show the world is... It's an oversimplification. And even what you showed me, back when we were together."

"Well, isn't that a neat trick that you managed to speak of it now, and yet you didn't say anything then."

"I always felt like there was a timer ticking down on what we had. I didn't want to clutter it up with unpleasant topics. And I never wanted to betray how much I cared. But I'm not a girl now. And while you may carry the weight of the fate of your nation on your shoulders, I carry the responsibility of taking care of our daughter. She is my primary concern, and she always will be. Lily is the most important thing in my universe. You must worry for millions. I worry for only one. And that means my focus is not split. I will defend her and her interest with all of me. Forever."

"And what about your own?"

"I am second. And I chose to be second when I committed to being her mother. When I knew that I wouldn't give her up. My father threw me out. He said I was an embarrassment. But it didn't matter. Because at that moment it ceased to be about me. It was about Lily, and me doing the best that I could for her. It was a free and wonderful realization, and it has been a free and wonderful way to live. And maybe...maybe this isn't what I want. I didn't sign on for this. For the life of public scrutiny, or to be…at the center of your engagement falling apart, which I can only imagine is going to make headlines everywhere."

"Yes. We are about to create something of an incident. I won't lie to you."

"I'm doing it for her."

Suddenly, he closed the distance between us, reaching out, his large hand cupping my cheek. He was like fire. His touch was a flame. And I had not expected that. I had thought that all those years would have given me a sort of immunity to the man, and yet there was none. "Is it?"

The words were husky, and his breath was warm and I could feel it across my lips.

It made me ache. Everywhere.

"Is it just for her?" he pressed. "You do not think that even a small part of yourself is going to find some enjoyment in this?"

My heart was thundering hard, so hard that I was convinced he could hear it. I swallowed.

I would not give him the satisfaction of seeing that he had shaken me. I would not let him come in and simply think that he could assume control of not only everything outside, but all the things inside me too. I had raised my daughter on my own for years. And yes, I was affected by him, but I would not simply give him the satisfaction of knowing that.

"Are you sure that this is entirely for your country?" I shot back. "And not you satisfying your thwarted hunter's instinct? You've caught me. And wasn't that what you wanted all those years ago?"

He growled and closed the distance almost entirely between us. And I faced the black fire, so close that I thought it might reduce me to ash. "No one leaves me," he gritted out. "No one abandons me."

"Don't they?"

I didn't know why I asked the question, or if it would have a particular sort of significance to him, but he released his hold on me, dropping his hand and turning away.

He raked his fingers through his black hair and then moved to face me again.

"Rearranging a wedding should not be too difficult. We have the venue. Guess all we need to do is change out the bride."

I gritted my teeth. "Just as I dreamed. From the time I was a little girl. That I might be a replacement bride for the Prince."

"She was your replacement."

The words were stunning. Rough, and for a moment I was certain that he had actually been speaking in a foreign language and my brain had translated them incorrectly. It took me a moment to realize that I hadn't been insulted in some way. Quite the contrary. He had admitted something to me that I didn't think he was happy to have spoken into existence.

"Well, then isn't it good that we put things to rights," I said. The words were barely above a whisper.

The problem was nothing felt put to rights at all. It all felt wrong and strange, deeply disconcerting.

And yet...

When he touched me, there was still heat. When he was near me, I still felt a kick of desire.

And if I was perfectly honest with myself, I would have been unhappy to go back home now.

No. That could not be. He could not have that kind of power over me. Never again.

I was not so weak that my attraction to Hercules could cause me to abandon reason.

"Perhaps we should toast," he said, lifting his glass. "To our union."

I raised my glass, my eyes never leaving his. It was a challenge, and I was not going to back down. Because I had changed. I had become someone different, forged in steel, in the fires of the conflagration that had occurred between us.

I had been a fool then. A girl easily wounded.

"This is for Lily," I said, more for myself than for him. "And our marriage is for Lily. It is not for us."

"Is that so?" he asked, his voice rough.

"Yes," I responded, pleased that I managed to keep my voice steady then.

It was the fire that terrified me. But more than that... it was the hope.

Because I could not seem to banish it no matter how much I tried.

"I don't care who you sleep with," I continued, the words catching in my throat. "But it won't be me."

"Excuse me?" The cold, dark ice in his tone sent a chill through me.

"We must be good parents to our daughter," I said. "Unless you're willing to drop down on your knees now and profess undying love, it won't work. We must be able to parent together, to exist together. To attend functions together and present a united front."

"My parents managed to do it for years. And trust me when I tell you they do not care much for each other."

"I am not your mother," I said. "And you are not your father. I'm confident of that, without ever having met either of them."

He stiffened. "Have it your way, Marissa. But I have to tell you I think your goals might be unrealistic here."

"Why?"

He smiled at me, and he didn't have to say a word, because electricity passed between us in that space, a switch flipped by the crook of his lips. And he knew it.

"We are not animals. We managed to go five years without touching one another, after all."

"True," he said, leaning in. "But that was when we were nowhere near each other. With an ocean between us it's quite easy to resist, is it not?" He reached out, the rough edge of his thumb resting against my upper lip. "But is it so easy to resist now? When I am here. And you still want me, so very much." My heart was tripping over itself, like the fool that I was, giddy and excited over the touch of this man.

"There is unfinished business between us," he continued.

"No," I whispered, calling on all of my strength and taking a step away from him. A step toward sanity.

"The business between us is Lily. And when she is finished, when she is grown, we will be too."

"Divorce then?" he asked. "How dull."

"It doesn't have to be divorce. We can simply separate. Whatever you need for your perfect royal image."

"You will not shame me by going out with other men," he said, the words shot through with iron.

I might have taken pleasure in the thought that he was jealous if I wasn't so desperate to release my hold on any sort of feelings for him. "I have no problem with that. I've managed just fine on my own this whole time."

"Have it your way, then." He downed the rest of the contents of his glass and took a step away from me, and I felt unaccountably cold when he did.

Then he removed his presence entirely from beside me.

"You might want to get some sleep. When we land, it will be morning in Pelion. And there will be much to attend to."

CHAPTER SIX

Hercules

OF THE MANY rebellions I had expected of Marissa, this refusal to be my wife in anything beyond name had thrown me off entirely.

It was one thing that I knew we could count on between us. Our passion.

Yes, we'd had an innocent relationship at first, but when passion had ignited between us it had been undeniable, unstoppable. We had traded in words for sighs of pleasure, and I had never regretted it. But this... This could not be endured.

I gritted my teeth. What man was this inside of me who could not handle being absent the touch of a particular woman? Since when had it ever mattered to me? I had more pressing matters to deal with than Marissa and her reluctance to be my bride in any real sense.

I had my father to deal with.

There was no question of having Marissa and Lily or Marissa's mother come to the palace.

Instead, I had them driven to my home that was nestled in the mountains of Pelion, on the opposite side of our major city from the palace.

My home was not a castle, but in many ways my father's home and mine had been set up like two warring palaces on opposing hills, facing each other down.

But now I was ready.

Ready to cross the gulf, ready to go to war.

I had steadied my hand; I had played at diplomacy. And I had done so in order to keep my father's wrath away from my mother and sister.

Though I knew at the moment neither of them were in residence in Pelion. They were in the French Riviera, as both of them preferred.

Even if not...

My father had already done the unforgivable.

He had kept me from my child.

I would not be civil.

I was given admittance into the palace immediately, and I walked directly through the glimmering obsidian halls down to the throne room.

It was Gothic, this palace. It always had been. As if the black heart of the Xenakis family resided at the center of this gilded mausoleum.

But then, I supposed it was true.

Whoever sat on the throne was the heart.

And my father had been up there spreading poison for far too long.

I would be better than the heart of this palace, than the heart of this nation.

I would be the brain.

That at least had a basis for reason. That at least had a code.

There were so many people who thought that the heart deserved to be followed. That the heart was the core of our humanity, but I knew the truth.

The heart could produce both humanity and un-speakable horror.

The heart was wicked. And it was deceptive. If you could find justification for your behavior deep in your heart, then a man could do anything.

However, reason would win out. I was confident in that. Reason I trusted in.

Reason I had violated only once.

With Marissa.

But it was funny how in the end she was the key to Pelion salvation. She had caused a shift in what was possible, and therefore a shift in my reasoning.

Something fascinating to be explored later, perhaps, but not when I was about to cross swords with my father.

I pushed the double doors of the throne room open without signaling my arrival.

The two Secret Service agents standing next to my father reached for their weapons, and I held up my hand. "Prince Hercules," I said.

"Prince Hercules," the other men repeated, nodding once.

"To what do I owe the pleasure?"

I had not been home in some time, and I was sur-prised by how diminished my father looked.

It was not just aging, for the Xenakis family tended to remain strong like oxen until the end. He looked weathered, and he looked weak, and my father was many things, but he had never been that.

"Have you climbed off of your latest whore long enough to see to issues of state?"

His voice was not frail, and apparently the meanness that coursed through his veins was well intact.

"I have been on a fact-finding mission," I said. "And I am not certain you will like what I uncovered."

"Is that so?"

The gleam in his eye seemed to swallow the light rather than give it off. Like the obsidian walls all around us.

That darkness was my legacy. And I would wield it against him happily now.

"Yes. Perhaps there is a secret that you forgot to tell me."

He did not look cowed by this; instead, he looked smug. "Oh, there are many, Hercules. Did you imagine all this time that you were sitting back pulling my strings and I never pulled yours? A common error of the youth. You think you know more. You think you know better. And because of that, you never take a moment to consider that I might be an opponent that is equal to you."

My lip curled. "I am not you," I said.

"That may be. But whether or not we are the same, we are an equal match."

"You're a monster."

"There are reasons that monsters live in caves for hundreds of years terrorizing the townspeople, and it isn't because they are stupid. You don't have to be good to win, Hercules. Perhaps you should remember that. If you're looking at your victory as an opportunity to measure the purity of your morality, I feel that might come to a disappointing end."

"Moral absolutism is not exactly at the core of what I've come to talk to you about. I found my child."

That I could see impacted him. "Have you?"

"Yes."

"Her mother was happy enough to sign away your rights for a payout."

"Because you made her think it was what I wanted. Marissa is a proud woman and she would no more beg me for anything, for my attention, than she would submit her child to a life on the streets."

Marissa's own words filled me, and I found I believed them with a great conviction in that moment.

"She is a woman of absolute strength and dignity, and she has done what we all should have done for the past years. She has raised Lily. Lily is the heir to the throne of Pelion. We owe her the same that we have owed every ruler that has come before her."

"A girl," my father sneered. "Of course you would produce a girl."

"She will be Queen. She will be Queen after me, and I daresay that whatever I don't manage to blot out that you brought on this country, she will erase entirely."

"Do you imagine I will step aside for you? For her?"

"You have to. Your birthday has passed. And I can see that age has begun to eat away at you."

He chuckled. "It is not age. But illness. It has long been said that I am too mean to die. I suspect soon we will see whether or not that is true."

"Step aside now."

"Have you not even a flicker of emotion for your father?"

"No," I said, "and you are not shocked. You concealed my child from me, and I have told you that I brought your granddaughter back to the country and you have no emotion to spare for that except disdain over her gender. No, I have no emotion to spare for you. None at all. You had none to spare for me. You had none to spare for her. I will stage a coup. We can end this in blood if you like."

"What if you didn't like the blood that was spilled?"

"If that is a threat against my family, I will end you now with my own hand."

"Do not speak of threats, Hercules, for we are more civilized than that, are we not? Political warfare is best waged with words and bureaucracy, don't you think?"

"The war is won. Engaging in a battle with you is a pointless waste of time. I marry Marissa in less than two weeks' time. The original wedding date stands. And upon that wedding you will abdicate."

"Will I?"

"Yes. Because if you don't, trust that I will make public what has occurred with Lily. Trust that I will destroy whatever fragment of a reputation you have left in this world. What do you want in the history books, Father? That in your current state is your primary concern anyway."

"I will require medical staff," he said. "I will require a residence."

"All to be provided," I said. "I will send you off with the most lavish of severance packages. You will want for nothing, and to all the world it will look as if the

Xenakis line has continued as it should. No one need know that I had to wrest it from you."

"If I resisted, what would you do?"

"I would have the military on my side, Father, and I think we both know it. No matter your threats, the blood that spilled would be yours."

My father was dying, and I knew that he was not fighting me because he wanted to extend his time as ruler, not when the tasks were clearly going to be too much for him and soon.

No, my father was fighting to avoid losing to me.

And that was why, whatever he said, I always would find victory.

Because I was not fighting a war of pettiness, but one for the people of my country.

"You have until the wedding to vacate this place. We will notify the Council that power is changing hands, and we will notify the press that my bride has changed. And we will come up with a suitable story for how I have only just now discovered my heir. And if you do anything that I do not care for in the meantime, that story will become more fact than fiction, and you will not like the results."

I considered how much I was counting on my father's ego to remain predictable as I made my way back to my home across the city.

He was a dying man, and many could argue he had nothing to lose. It was true enough. But for my father, legacy would always count in the end.

I wondered if it occurred to him that I had control of that legacy. Because whatever I told him while he drew breath I could change once he was gone.

The ultimate tragedy for a man who sought to control everything in his life, I supposed. A man who did not think he had to give deference to a son who was beneath him.

Not even my father could manipulate death. And once he was gone, he would have power over nothing.

The house on the hill was not my home.

I had never given much thought to homes.

The castle had always felt very much like my father's domain, and like it was sadly tainted by the sins of the previous generations.

One thing my father would get to live to see, and it gave me an extreme amount of pleasure, was the joy that our people would feel when he was finally removed from the throne.

My wedding would be a cause for celebration in a way no one had anticipated.

And—something I had not thought of—Marissa would be a welcome bride, even though she was not from Pelion, by sheer virtue of the fact that she was the method by which my father was uninstalled.

In contrast to the darkness of the palace, my home was made of light. Windows and stark walls, and white marble on the floors.

Not because I was a creature of virtue so much as even devils got tired of hell.

I was so used to my staff being invisible and everything being in a certain order that the disruption in the white—Marissa's figure and Lily's small one—gave me pause.

"You're back," she said.

"Yes," I said, battling against the warring responses

to the sight of both of them that were occurring in my body. There was an ache when I looked at Lily and I did not know what to call it.

I *knew* what I felt for Marissa.

And I disliked very much the sensation that she was holding the most vulnerable part of me in her hand and guiding me around by it.

If she wanted to do that, she had to give me pleasure, rather than just attempts to manipulate.

"Have you not found everything to your liking?"

"Lily wanted to see more of the house," Marissa said.

"It's the biggest house I've ever seen. Is it the castle?" Lily asked.

"No," I said, working to gentle my tone. "We will move into the castle after the…after the wedding."

Lily's eyes were shining. "You're going to marry my mom."

"Yes," I said. "And she will be a princess too."

Lily was enraptured, clearly captured by what to her felt like a real-life fairy tale. She wrapped her arms around her mother's leg. "We'll be princesses together," she said.

Marissa, for her part, tried to force a smile and patted Lily on the back. "Yes. We will."

"Can I go and get Nana?"

"Sure," Marissa responded.

Lily bounded up the stairs, her dark curls bouncing behind her.

"What were you doing?" Marissa asked.

"You don't care what I was doing," I said. "Remember, I have permission to be with anyone I choose at any time I choose. Your edict, Marissa, not mine."

"It was not a question of where your private parts were, Hercules, but your person."

"I was speaking to my father," I said. "And somehow I managed not to kill him." I made my way over to the bar that sat in the corner of the living area and I poured myself some scotch. Crutches be damned, some things were better done with alcohol.

"I see."

"It has never been a secret to me that he was a monster. But he kept my child from me, Marissa, and I cannot forgive that. I will not."

"Why should you? If you had come back into my life simply telling me you had changed your mind… If you had known about Lily all this time, I would not have forgiven you. There are some things that are simply unforgivable."

I thought of her, as she had been. Young and pregnant and alone. And for the first time, I could see clearly enough through my rage to truly think of her as a victim.

I had cast her in the role of defector for so many years. And then the shock of discovering that I had a child had…

It had undone my world.

And then it had put it back together with strange and new possibilities, and I had not been able to ignore the political implications.

"I'm going to need you," I said.

Because it did no good for me to dwell on the past. On what might have been, and who she was to me. On how terrified she must have been. Alone and…heartbroken.

It didn't sit well with me.

When I had touched her, I had known that I had crossed a boundary I normally would not.

Virgins were not something I had ever cared to trifle with before. There were too many unintended consequences.

But I had decided on some level that I would make Marissa mine, and so I had justified it.

And then, when she abandoned me, I had recast her in my mind in the role of scarlet woman somehow, even though I knew full well that she had never known the touch of a man before me.

Marissa.

No, there was no point in thinking of her that way. It was better to focus on now.

"Need me for what?"

"We have to speak to the press."

"Why do you need me for that?"

"Because. Because I need to put a face to my new bride, for all the world to see. Because there is going to be an interest."

"I'm exhausted," she said.

"And we are getting married in two weeks' time. Sleep now if you can. Try to catch up. Tomorrow, they will be here."

"In the house? I don't want Lily on camera."

"You understand that is impractical. Lily will be on camera from now on to the rest of her life. She is going to be a public figure. An object of interest and curiosity. It is far better that we have Lily on camera when we decide. Far better that we have official photographers taking her photos. It will be better, trust me."

"I... But she's very little. And this is all very new."

"Tomorrow I will only need you. But you will have to look the part. And whatever your personal feelings on me or the subject...you will have to look as if you can bear my touch."

The air went thick between us, and she captured her lower lip between her teeth. Worrying it.

I reached out and then dropped my hand quickly. I had been about to touch her. But I refused.

I would not allow her that kind of power. I would not allow her that kind of control.

Everything had been put in motion. By my hand.

I had the power here, not her.

We would both do well to remember it.

CHAPTER SEVEN

Marissa

I SLEPT TERRIBLY. I kept waiting for Lily to crawl into my bed, because I was certain that the new environment would be uncomfortable for her, but she didn't come.

And when I woke up early in the morning, unable to stand staying in bed any longer, I tiptoed down the hall to her room and found her sleeping like the little princess she was in the middle of a giant king-size bed. She barely made a dent in the feather mattress; her dark hair spilled over the pillow.

She felt happy here. She felt safe. I was the one with the issue.

But then, I was the one who had a history with Hercules.

I sighed heavily and padded down the stairs, searching for coffee. I kept waiting to see Hercules. But he didn't materialize.

And when the sun finally came up, I could see the breathtaking view out the window. The craggy, glorious mountains all around limned with gold. And below...

The sea. The glorious Mediterranean burning like a jewel in the early morning.

This place was beautiful.

It would be my home.

I could see the ocean.

The wave of relief I felt at that realization surprised me.

Lily and I were near enough to the water in Boston. We didn't have a view, but we could easily walk down to the harbor.

Even so, sometimes I ached for the beautiful simplicity of the shorelines in Medland. The bristling seagrass that grew from the soft sand hills and the rich blue water.

This was different. But it was so close. The sea as if it was illuminated from its center.

My heart felt inexplicably tied to the ocean.

And it made sense suddenly that it was by the ocean I had first seen Hercules.

I stood out on the balcony, looking down over the water for an untold amount of time, until I heard the sound of footsteps behind me.

It still wasn't Hercules.

It was a woman, immaculately dressed, her hair and makeup flawless.

"You must be Marissa?" She spoke with faintly accented English, her voice gloriously cultured. "I am Isabella. I'm here to help you get dressed for the press conference."

It turned out that Isabella's statement was an understatement. She was not there simply to help me get dressed, but to acquaint me with an entirely new wardrobe that she had selected sometime between the moment I had been whisked away from Medland and when we landed in Pelion.

We set aside multiple items to be altered and chose one formfitting red dress that fell past my knees and was cut classically, that needed only a bare minimum of sewing sorcery. Isabella accomplished it in moments. Then she did some expert styling on my hair, promising that I needed a bit of salon time and would get it later on.

She also did makeup, miraculous things with it—things that I hadn't known were possible.

With a bit of shading, she made my face look narrower, more sharply defined, and with some glue and fake lashes made my eyes look stunningly wide.

"Camera ready," she said.

I turned and looked in the mirror, feeling shocked by what I saw. "That doesn't look like me."

"It doesn't have to. It has to look like a princess."

I recognized the truth of that. It wasn't meant to be insulting, not in any way. It was simply the truth.

Hercules needed to present a woman to the country—to the world—who was believable. Who could be likable enough to smooth over the narrative that was going to have to be spun about the existence of Lily.

Come to think of it, I didn't even know what that narrative was going to be. And I still hadn't seen Hercules. So we had not had a chance to talk about it.

As soon as Isabella was finished, she whisked me out of my bedroom and down the stairs. And then suddenly she was gone, and Hercules was there.

"We will be meeting the members of the press out in the courtyard."

His eyes flicked over me, and I saw heat there that made my skin feel like it was prickling.

"She's done a good job."

"Yes," I responded.

"We will tell them you did not know my identity, and I didn't know about Lily, and it was only recently when headlines of my engagement hit the news that you realized who I was. You came to me, not to destroy my wedding, but to make sure that I knew about my daughter. And that was when we decided it would be best if we were together."

It was so close to the truth, and it made my heart twist. I should be happy with that. That it wasn't an outright lie. But…

"It's not exactly a story that will sweep people away."

"What do you want?"

"It's not about what I want," I said. "But…people want to know. They'll want to dig in deep. And I… It all sounds so practical, and there's nothing beautiful to weave from it. People want to weave a story."

"We are marrying for practical reasons."

"Yes," I said softly. "But don't you think it would be more impacting if you said that when I came to find you, you realized that… I was what you had been missing all along?"

The words tasted so strange on my lips, almost like honey, and a surge of longing welled up inside of me, and worse, hope.

Hope was a beast inside me I could not seem to banish.

"I like that," he said. "I'll use it. You're right. It is

much more compelling. Unfortunately, not much can be done for Vanessa's feelings."

"Did she love you?"

He shook his head. "No. I don't believe so. She will be angry that she isn't going to be Queen. On that you can trust me. It has been a goal of hers most of her life. She has always known that she was the most suitable woman in all the land for the heir apparent."

"Bloodlines."

"Bloodlines," he said. "They are all important when you are royal."

"For all that my father was difficult, and there were things that he…that he did and said that I feel were wrong… I was taught that people were more than blood. That we are spiritual. That our souls are what truly matter. This idea of blood overshadowing everything is so foreign to me."

"It's a lovely concept," he said. "That a human being's spiritual self might matter more than, say, who his father was. But in my experience that is simply not the case. Man is a physical being. He wants power. Above all else. And the best way to consolidate that is with money. And then you can make rules. Any rules you like. About how the power can only be passed down through blood. When a man is hungry, he eats. When he desires a woman, he finds physical release with her. When he is tired, he sleeps."

"And what does he do when he is sad? What does he do when he's lonely? When he has a fear, or a hope or a dream, who does he confide in? And when he finds satisfaction for those things, what does it feed? His body? Or his soul?"

"I don't believe in what I can't see. What I cannot touch."

"That's very sad."

"Everything else is simply the way man builds justi- fication for things. All manner of things. We dress our selfish desires up as matters of the heart, as dreams and callings... Morality can be lost much easier than when we view the world through black-and-white terms."

"Well, for the purposes of the press conference, per- haps we should borrow from my philosophy more than yours."

"I believe it likely we should."

I didn't know why the conversation with him made me sad and happy all at the same time. It reminded me a bit of the kinds of talks we used to have down by the shore. All kinds of things.

Ideas that challenged my view on the world and on myself.

But there hadn't been an edge to him then, not like this. It was as if he'd let his guard down with me then, rather than wrapping his every word in hardened cyni- cism.

I studied his face. There were new lines there. Grooves that had settled in by his mouth, by his eyes, just in the years since I had seen him.

I wanted to will them away. To will him back in time.

But I couldn't. And I knew it.

But we were in the here and now, and he was propel- ling me out the door and toward the courtyard. It was beautiful, flagstone and vivid green grass, surrounded by glorious flowering bushes.

The security detail was there, and a limited number of press members had arrived as well.

"We will stand in the front. You will stand beside me. You do not need to speak. I will do the talking."

And then I was following him, right into the public eye. I stood beside him, my hands clasped in front of me as I had seen any number of political wives do at press conferences over the years. I did my best to mimic that pose. That smile, and those rigid, resolute shoulders that they seemed required to possess, whatever their husband might be confessing to.

"I thank you for coming today for this announcement. I appreciate that it is a bit unorthodox. But it seemed the best way to proceed. After I am done speaking, I will give the opportunity for three members of the press to ask a question. And only one question. Then we will be done, and you will be escorted from the premises."

I could feel the need to ask questions radiating from the people in the audience, but they all seemed too afraid to do anything out of turn.

"To begin with, my marriage will still proceed on the appointed date. But I have an important announcement regarding the bride. Vanessa and I will no longer be getting married. Instead, I am marrying Ms. Marissa Rivero of Medland, Massachusetts."

To those who didn't know, that might make it sound as if I had a pedigree. Medland was known for being the preferred second, third or fourth home location of the rich, connected and political. But anyone who truly understood would know that if I was from Medland, I was not one of those people.

If you were well-off, you spent summers there. You didn't live there.

You certainly weren't from there.

"I knew Marissa years ago, and we had a romance," he continued, yet again being very careful with his wording. "Due to the delicate nature of my position, I did not reveal to her who I was, and she was not aware. When our relationship was cut short during a time when I had to return to Pelion, she could not locate me, and when I returned to find her, I could not locate her. Over the course of years, she discovered who I was, and was only recently able to establish contact. When she did, I discovered that she'd had my child."

The members of the press couldn't help it—a wave of shock went through them, and chatter rose up in the serene garden.

Hercules held his hand up. And as if he'd roared, they silenced. "I'm not finished. When she found me, not only was I overjoyed to discover that I was a father, but I also found I was overjoyed to be reconnected with her. It was a relationship that I…was never ready to let go of. And I knew that I could not let her get away from me again. It is with great regret that I broke my engagement to Vanessa off, but she understands the extraordinary circumstances that were at play."

The crowd shifted, and scattered observers began to stand, lurching forward, questions competing with each other to exit their mouths first.

"I'm not finished," he said again, and again, the crowd stilled. "Further, on the date of our marriage, I will be crowned King of Pelion. Marissa will be my consort, and that is the final word on it."

They all stood frozen, like dogs on the hunt waiting to be given the command. They didn't want to incur a scolding from him yet again, Marissa assumed. The disapproval of Hercules Xenakis was a powerful thing.

He inclined his head. "Now you may speak."

They all jostled for position, raising their hands and hurling out queries. But Hercules pointed to one.

"This question is for Ms. Rivero," the first man said.

I didn't know that I would be asked questions, and I wasn't certain if it was allowed, but Hercules did not deny them, so I turned my focus to the reporter. "Did you track him down finally solely because he was getting married?"

My tongue felt thick and my heart was pounding hard. I didn't have experience speaking in front of people. I'd even avoided it in church, during prayer or when we'd been asked to share good news in our lives.

But this was for Lily.

I would be a reflection on her, and I had to deal with my nerves, I had to deal with my reservations, my issues, because they would rebound onto her. It couldn't be helped.

"Yes and no," I said. Which was true enough. "I had no other way of getting in contact with him. But his location for his celebration before the wedding was revealed. And so I was able to approach him. And I was able to tell him…to tell him about our daughter. The timing is unfortunate, I know, but believe me, if I had been able to tell him sooner, I would have done."

Hercules looked at me, the expression in his dark eyes unreadable. Unknowable. I would have given much to be able to see into his mind. "There is a duty that a man in my position must assume for his country. A responsibility. Making Lily legitimate is part of that responsibility. She is my heir, and the future ruler of this country. Therefore, whatever speculation you might want to apply to Marissa's motives, you should know that the right thing was done here. What sort of man would I be, what sort of King would I be, if I ignored my child? If I refused to recognize her, to grant her the legitimacy that she requires. What sort of man would I be if I replaced my heir with another simply to avoid making waves? What would that mean for her? Indeed, for the fate of a nation. But quite beyond that... A man might have responsibilities, but a man has a heart as well. And when I saw Marissa again, I knew that I could not ignore mine."

I was shocked by the words that had come out of his mouth, for they were in direct opposition to the sort of thing that he had said to me just before we came out here. He wrapped his arm around my waist and then he was pulling me to him. And I couldn't breathe. I couldn't think. All I could do was feel. All I could do was breathe him in. Him. Hercules.

My greatest triumph and my greatest sin.

The man who had made me a woman. In so many different ways. More ways than just the simple euphemism that was often used for that phrase. No. It was his attention that had given me strength. His touch that had made me wild, and his betrayal that had made me fearless.

And now it was his hand on my chin making my heart beat so fast that I thought I might fall over.

When he claimed my mouth with his, it was like the

world exploded. Brilliant bursts of light behind my eyes that left me trembling, shaking.

His mouth was like I remembered it. Warm and firm, but so much better now for all the years of separation.

Like going home.

I had just returned home after a five-year absence, and it had not been like this.

It was as if I'd been struggling with a door for years, and he'd handed me the key to the lock, only to have it click in place and turn easily.

I felt walls collapse inside of me. Walls that had been protecting me. That had been closing off so much in the way of feeling.

Of being a woman.

I had become Lily's mother. And when I had taken that role on, I had assumed it entirely. I had made myself forget. I had made myself forget the rude insanity of what had caused my change in identity in the first place.

I had done it deliberately. And I had done it well.

But it had only been sleeping. It had not been banished.

That mouth.

He parted my lips with his, sliding his tongue against mine, and that was not for the press, I knew. Because a kiss to the mouth would've been just fine without increasing the intimacy.

He had done that for me.

To show me. To show me that no matter what I said I still wanted him.

Of course, I had known that already. I didn't need his games as a reminder.

It was why I had told him that we would not be having a physical relationship in the first place.

Because I understood that in that equation I was the one who was vulnerable. I was the one who would be wounded.

But right now, I was just the one on fire.

And I was gladly allowing myself to burn.

His hands were large and warm, pressed in the space between my shoulder blades, holding me firmly. He was such a breathless temptation. And I wanted to give in. I remembered all too well how it felt. To leap off the edge of reason and into his beautiful obsidian abyss.

It took me minutes—at least it seemed so to me—to realize that I was making a fool of myself on a public stage. I was melting in the arms of this man for all the world to see.

But I couldn't pull away, because we were being watched. Because this was the moment he'd warned me about.

It was for show.

It was for show.

That doused some of that fire in me.

It wasn't that Hercules wanted me so. He wanted to drive the point home to the press that what he'd done he did out of duty and love, to instill in his people a sense of confidence that he was a ruler who would do things in a much more measured way than his father.

When we parted, he still held me, his arm around my waist.

And he took a breath. Just one, but it was ragged at the edges, and it gave me the hope that he had not been unaffected by what had passed between us.

I shouldn't care.

I truly shouldn't care.

"So you see," he said, his voice slightly lower. Slightly rougher. "There is duty, and then there is something that goes beyond it. It would've been a grave misstep for me to carry on with my engagement to Vanessa, even though it would have been the path of least resistance. But I'm not a man who takes the path of least resistance. I'm a man who acts for the best interests of all those involved. And I am a man who will do more than simply lead clinically, as has been done before me.

"And I will make change where change must be made. To ensure that the citizens of Pelion are living with freedom and are not being shut out of the comforts which the royal family has enjoyed without them for far too long. I hope, if you can, that you will see these actions I've taken now as an indicator of who I am, and that you will find it to be positive."

Another reporter stood up.

"No further questions," Hercules said.

"You said we got three," the man said.

"I did," Hercules confirmed. "I have changed my mind. And as I told you, I reserve the right to do so."

And then he whisked me away from the reporters, and from the clamor behind us, ushering me back into the house.

I had to lean against the wall for strength, my energy suddenly draining out of me as if those questions had punctured a hole in me. And I told myself it was because all of this was overwhelming. Not because Hercules himself was overwhelming.

"You did well," he said, his dark eyes appraising me,

but I saw it there. That he wasn't unaffected. And my own heart tripped over in response.

"The wedding is in two weeks' time," he said. "I have no doubt you'll be prepared for it."

"I'm glad you don't have any doubt, because I... We don't really know each other, Hercules. We had stolen time together away from both of our real lives. I'm a pastor's daughter who never left the island the whole time I was growing up. I wasn't thrust into the real world until after I had Lily... And I had to become so...so hard to protect myself. To protect her. To stop myself from missing what I'd left behind so much that I ached. All the time. And you... All of this is yours. It's your legacy. But it isn't mine."

"But it is Lily's," he said, his voice firm. "And that you are bringing yourself into it so she can have it is a great thing you've done."

I was floored by the compliment. "That might be the first nice thing you've said about my parenting."

"I've had time to accept that what you did... You had no other choice. That it was my father who did this to us. Not you."

"It's forced you to have empathy."

"I wouldn't call it that. I would simply say that there is no logical way to look at it that casts you as a villain, Marissa, and I am a man of logic, always willing to be corrected if a more reasonable scenario presents itself."

"Well, I'm happy that my villain status seemed unreasonable to you."

"There is much to be done in the lead-up to the wedding. Much diplomacy to be handled, seeing as I am assuming the throne the day of the wedding, and there will be policy ready to be enacted upon the exact hour. I will not see much of you over this time."

It was a relief, though I didn't tell him that. "Okay. I think I can handle that. Since I haven't seen much of you over the past five years."

"Lily will be the flower girl for the wedding."

My heart squeezed tight. Because somewhere in all this was a mixed-up fantasy of what I had dreamed would happen all this time, even if it hadn't been a conscious dream. That my Prince had come, even if he was late. That our daughter would share in our special day.

Except, it was not our special day. It was Lily's, perhaps. It was the kingdom of Pelion's. And those were good things. But the last thing it was about was myself and Hercules. And, no matter how incendiary a kiss between us might be, I had to remember that.

If I didn't, I was in danger of breaking all over again.

And I wasn't sure that I had it in me to emerge stronger the second time. I didn't know if I would be able to emerge at all.

"In two weeks," I said, nodding my head purposefully and turning away from him.

Because I had to turn away. Because I had to be strong.

Because none of this was for me.

And it never would be.

CHAPTER EIGHT

Hercules

THE DAY OF the wedding, of the coronation, dawned bright and clear. My father was nowhere to be seen, and I was not unhappy with that. I was told by members of staff that he had gone up to his new home—a lavish keep nestled in the mountains—and would likely not be coming down.

It was fine by me, and I would be making an announcement regarding the King's health for the benefit of the media.

I was ready.

Ready for all of this to be cemented. Ready for it to be over.

We had settled into a pattern at my home, the four of us. Lily chattered and filled the awkward spaces that existed between the adults, and Marissa's mother had assumed an easy and content position nannying the child. Marissa had been undergoing a crash course in the customs and laws of the country, and what duties were required of a royal spouse.

Meanwhile I had made sure that every piece was in

place for an easy transition of power and that I could swiftly repudiate the prohibitive laws my father had placed that kept the people in poverty.

Change what happened. And I knew that change would not be instantaneous, but it would be as close to it as possible under my watch.

And Lily would bear witness to it. To the changes that a good ruler would make, and I had confidence that she would make changes of her own. Her sweet nature—which seemed natural to her—surprised me at every turn.

And it made me wonder if she would have turned out half so well at this point in time if she had been raised with me.

There was something in that child—a lightness— that was not in me. And I knew that it could have only come from Marissa.

I wouldn't see Marissa until she actually began to walk down the aisle, but I did see Lily, dressed all in white, with ribbons woven through her dark hair and a basket of flowers in her hand. She lit up, and she ran to me, opening her arms.

And the sight was enough to bring me to my knees.

I did not understand how this worked. I had never cared for children much at all. I didn't dislike them, but they weren't often in my presence. My sister had been born when I was fifteen, but my father had never allowed me much interaction with her.

But every fiber of my being responded to this child, and I knew beyond a shadow of a doubt that I would wage war for her.

Essentially, I had. And it had nothing to do really

with fairness to her. Everything to do with the fact that I wanted her. She was my child, and I wanted her as mine. I could not go on in a world where I knew she existed and pretended that she did not. An emotional revelation for a man like me, especially one who had a father such as mine.

Every so often that terrified me.

Because wanting just for the sake of it was a dangerous sort of drug. The beginning of all those outrageous justifications that my father himself engaged in.

A man had to act from a more morally superior place than his own soul. And I knew that well.

My father acted from a place of using his own desires as guidance, and he had not been a good father.

I might not know how to be one either, but one thing I knew for sure: I did not want to be like him.

"Daddy," Lily said, "do you like my dress?"

I was frozen. I didn't know quite what to do or say. "Yes," I said, the word sticking in my throat.

"It's good for twirling." She spun in a circle happily, and the freedom and simplicity with which she did things struck me. Because while I was contemplating the future of the country, of my humanity, just before my wedding to Marissa, Lily was spinning circles.

I had never been a carefree child. I had not been allowed. I wondered how different I might have been...

But then, there was no point mourning the loss of childlike joy.

What I had become was what was needed for Pelion, for my people, my country. And I would honor my responsibilities.

Right now, that responsibility included seeing to Lily's happiness.

That was a logical choice.

I liked what Marissa had built in her. And I could see how she was the future of Pelion.

I could see that I would have to work at being a softer parent than my own had been.

That satisfied me because it was a logical conclusion that would put me in a position where I would not crush my daughter's spirit. The very thought of crushing my Lily made my chest feel like it was so tight I couldn't breathe.

I moved to my position at the front of the church, and I looked around. It was amazing, the number of people that had come for this. Who were looking to the future of Pelion. We were all done with business as it had been conducted under my father's reign. So many of the people in my country didn't even know life out from under his thumb. But it would change.

It was all changing today.

And I kept my thoughts on the state of the country as music began to play. As my daughter came down the aisle with her flower petals and a grin on her face to light up the entire church.

And then the music changed, and the spectators stood. And I knew beyond a shadow of a doubt that if it had been Vanessa I was waiting for, if it had been Vanessa concealed by those double doors, my chest would not be locked up like there was a rock directly in the center of it. I knew. I knew. I knew.

But as it was, I found that I could not breathe.

That kiss…

Two weeks ago, my lips had touched Marissa's for the first time in years. And I remembered.

Remembered why that particular spark was an insanity that transcended all else. I remembered why I had been willing to overturn cars, my life, anything in order to get another taste of the passion that was between us. A passion that was unlike anything else I had ever experienced. Marissa. An intoxicating flavor unlike any other. I needed it like none I had ever known before.

And then those doors parted, and it was like the sun had been let into that old stone building.

She was an angel. An angel of light come down into hell with me.

I was going to take her back to that glittering obsidian palace, full of darkness and soaked in centuries of despair.

And I did not even regret it. How could I? How could I win this vision of beauty that was mine to capture? Mine to hold an ethereality just short of heaven that had fallen down to earth so that I might pick her up and conceal her in all that darkness.

The dress was a cloud, falling effortlessly over her body, swirling around her legs with each step she took. The neck was square and low, revealing a tantalizing amount of her beautiful curves.

Her dark hair was pulled back, wisps of curls cascading around her face.

I was thankful that the makeup for the wedding day was more natural than what she'd had the day of the press conference. She had been beautiful—she was always beautiful—but I had missed that familiar beauty.

As she drew closer, she filled my vision, made the edges of the view before me go fuzzy, until it was only her I saw.

For three years I had seen only Marissa.

So this was a familiar state for me.

But not a comfortable one.

And she thought that we would not consummate this marriage.

I reached out, and she took my hand.

It was trembling.

I was cast back to that first time we'd been together on the beach in Medland.

She'd been a virgin, and I had ached with a strange sense of humility.

That she had given her body to me. That she had done so with joy, in spite of her nerves.

I had never known such a feeling. I had never been given such a gift.

I was struck with the parallels between that moment and this. This vision in white walking toward me like a virgin sacrifice.

But she was not a virgin.

And she was not giving herself as a gift.

I had to remember that.

I had not told her about what was to happen after the wedding. She would not be happy.

But the decision had been made, and I had not consulted her. She would have to get used to such things.

The vows felt like they had an especially heavy weight to them. Perhaps because I was promising myself to her for the sake of a nation and promising myself to the nation as well. And to Lily. Because the vows were a tangle of vines around the both of us, and so many other things.

But then, nothing else mattered. Because then it was time for me to kiss her again. And it consumed me.

When the minister gave the command, I was more than ready. And it didn't matter to me that we were in a church, or that we had onlookers. All that mattered was her.

I cupped her face with my hands, and the silk of her skin made me shudder. I leaned in, inhaling the scent of her. Her beauty. Her perfection.

Her.

And then I tasted her.

Slowly at first, encouraging her to part her lips for me that I might taste her even deeper.

And she obeyed.

I would feast on her, except that I knew I would not be able to gorge myself entirely on her beauty because there were limits to what could be expressed here and now. So I ended the kiss, with much more regret than I care to admit.

We were then pronounced man and wife, and immediately after I took bonding vows to become the King, as she vowed to be consort and, like myself, put the kingdom of Pelion before all else.

It was a funny thing, but as she took the vows, I knew that they were a lie. She would not put the kingdom above all else, because she would always place Lily above anything else in the world. And I found a measure of satisfaction in that. Because whatever my feelings, they would not be hers. She would be the one who compensated for all my shortcomings. And I would rule. As I should. As I must.

When it was done, I bent down and picked Lily up from the ground, holding her, and she clung to me as if it were the most natural thing in the world.

It was not. Not for me, still not. But that it was for her was one of the more revelatory things I had ever experienced.

We would do official portraits later, but for now, these would be the first photographs together of us as the royal family.

Family.

It was one of those words that was thrown around often enough, though in my family, it was more likely that you would hear about blood. Blood, that most important of connectors, that essential component that made a person, and/or Royal, worthy or not in the eyes of my father.

It meant something different to me in that moment, and I could not credit why, which was added to the list of unsettling things I'd been grappling with for the past two weeks.

There were postwedding celebrations planned, but we would not attend them. It was not customary for a royal couple to do so. They would either retire to small, private parties, or they would do as we were about to do.

I set Lily down, taking hold of her hand, and we walked down the aisle together.

Marissa's mother, who had been seated in the front row, joined us, and when we were in a private room at the back of the church, I knelt down in front of my daughter. "Will you be all right staying with Nana for the next week?"

Lily frowned. "What?"

"We are going to move from the big house into the palace," I said. "But it will take some time." Some of that to do with the fact that I was having every piece of my father's legacy removed from the place.

"And your mother and I are going on a honeymoon."

Marissa sputtered, "You didn't say anything about a honeymoon."

"I know I didn't, because I suspected you would fight me. But this is not something worth having a fight over, my Queen. It is a tradition among royal families that we retreat to the private island for this period of time away from the spotlight, away from all others. It has been prepared for our arrival, and there is no question of whether or not we will go."

"You would have gone with Vanessa?" she asked, and I was surprised at how quickly she reversed the immediate spark of rage in her eye.

"Yes," I responded. "I would have. As tradition dictates."

"Our agreement stands."

I cast a glance at my new mother-in-law. "Our agreement stands," I said, and I wonder if her mother had any idea what that agreement was.

I gritted my teeth, because of course I could not help but imagine demolishing that resolve of hers.

"You might have asked me," she said.

"Did you have other plans?" I asked.

Perhaps not the best tone to take immediately with one's mother-in-law looking on, but I was King, after all.

"You know I didn't," she said.

"You and Lily will have free run of the house while the palace is being prepared," I said to her mother. "When Marissa and I return, we will all go together."

"Are you all right?" her mother asked.

"I'm fine," Marissa responded. "If not blissfully happy."

It was all quite a bit much in the way of family connection for me. Given that I had been raised by wolves essentially. Blue blood notwithstanding.

"We must go," I said.

"Now?"

Marissa suddenly looked terrified.

"Is that a problem?"

"I've never left Lily."

Lily patted her mother's arm pragmatically. "You'll be back," she said.

Marissa looked stunned.

"Yes," she responded, looking down at her daughter with wide eyes.

"And I'll be with Nana," Lily said.

"Yes again," came Marissa's reply.

"Then it's settled," I said.

"Do I have to go in this dress?"

"No, don't be silly. I've had your going-away outfit selected for you."

"What is it?"

"Something befitting a honeymoon on a private island."

CHAPTER NINE

Marissa

I WAS MARRIED, and I was a queen.

And still, my predominant concern was the fact that I was going to a private island dressed in a very brief gold dress that left little to the imagination with a man who I was going to have a very hard time resisting if he put his mind to doing any sort of seducing.

I felt the strangest things in that moment, and I had no idea what to do with them. I was...sad and terrified and filled with guilt at leaving Lily, but there was also a strange sense of exhilaration inside of me.

I hadn't spent even one night apart from Lily since I'd given birth four years earlier. I didn't know what it meant to be away from her. And now I was going to a private island for a week with only this man for company. No responsibilities. Nothing.

It was an invitation to the kind of sin that I had only gotten a taste of all that time ago. If only things weren't so complicated.

Being pampered the last couple of weeks had reminded me...that I was a woman.

Kissing Hercules twice in the last couple of weeks had reminded me that I was a woman.

Not just a mother. Not just a caregiver. But a woman. One who was sensual, and who had…needs, whether or not I had tried to suppress them. And I had tried.

Lily was well cared for, and the island was certain to be beautiful, and if it wasn't for the fact that I didn't trust myself, everything would be fine.

But Hercules was so big, so hot and hard and beautiful, and I had been reminded yet again today when he had kissed me at the wedding. But at least then I'd had layers of wedding gown in between our bodies, and now I had been reduced to the flimsy article made of netting and gems, and it felt like his heat, his body, was that much closer to mine.

"How come you stayed in a tux?" I asked as our plane touched the ground.

"Because you didn't choose anything for me."

The grin that he treated me to was wicked, almost light, and it made my heart lift, because I had not seen him look like that in…

A long time.

"Can you really leave for a week after being crowned King?"

"Yes. Everything necessary to create a smooth transition was put into place some time ago. And I knew that I would be away. Everything is set in motion. And we are a twenty-minute plane ride away. It's not as if we can't return home quickly if need be."

Considering that Lily was on another island, it was a comforting thought. "There was no one else here," he said, as the door to the plane opened.

"Well," I said, "the pilot is here for now."

"He will be leaving with the plane."

He stepped out of the door and held his hand out toward me, his right foot on the second stair. "Come with me."

I had taken his hand once before, and I had followed him wherever it led. I would be foolish to do it again, and yet I found myself grasping on to him, allowing him to usher me down the steps.

The surroundings were beautiful. Breathlessly so. This island was a rough-cut gem in the middle of the Mediterranean, without another soul or another building in sight. I hadn't realized that a place like this might exist. Or that it would be part of Hercules's legacy. He was so urbane, so very smooth, that I had imagined him out of place on the small island of Medland. Even though it was a sophisticated old-world form of rural living, he had seemed like a fish out of water there. But now I wondered.

There was a car parked partway across the runway, and he led us toward it.

"We will take this," he said. "The house is across the island."

"On a mountain?"

"Naturally," he responded.

"Do rich people live on mountains just for the views?"

"Well, yes, and to remind others of their place in the world. How will people get the full sense of how above them we are if we don't place our houses up off the ground?"

"Good point," I said. "But there are other ways to

lord superiority over people. To make them feel small. My father was an expert at doing it through religion."

"Your father threw you out," he said.

"Yes. When he found out about Lily."

We got into the car and he began to drive.

The scenery outside the window was stunning, lush trees and bright pink flowers with the clear breathtaking sea beyond.

"Your father died," he said, clearly intent on pushing this line of personal conversation.

"Yes," I responded.

"And that's why you were able to reconnect with your mother."

"Yes. She sneaked away to see us sometimes. She lied to him. He controlled her, but…not in the way he thought he did. He…he was terrible. He was a man who liked power more than he loved God. Believe me when I tell you that. And people trusted him… They… I did too. I trusted what he had to say because I didn't know any better. I believed that I had no other choice but to feel guilty all of my life because there was something wrong with me. You don't need money to make people feel small. But in the end… In the end, when you live a life like my father did, I don't know that you leave a lot of people behind to mourn you. More than anything, I mourn what could have been."

"Do you?"

"I mean, I try not to. But sometimes I wonder what it might have been like if we had a different relationship. But then I realize he would've had to be a different man altogether. And that's impossible. I had the relationship with my father he was capable of having. It's sad, but it's true. And there's ultimately nothing that can be done."

"As long as my father is in the history books in the way that he wants to be, he will be happy." He laughed. "I'm not sure how he'll know, but…maybe the view from hell is clear."

I rubbed my chest, but didn't say anything more. After that I didn't need to anyway, because the house came into view. I had thought I was quite past having my breath taken away, but apparently I wasn't.

Apparently, there were still levels of luxury that could shock me.

This house seemed to be made entirely of glass, set into the mountain, facing the sea. If his home in Pelion was beautiful, then this was otherworldly.

The inside was even more amazing, the pale coastal light bathing everything in a glow. Everything was white, as it was in his home.

"You know, this really is an impractical color scheme for children."

"Children?" He arched a dark brow and looked at me.

And for the first time, I saw the future. A possible future, anyway, one that wounded me and lifted me in ways that I could not begin to describe.

Children. Plural. I had not meant to say that, but it was all too easy to imagine.

The two of us having more children, together. Having him with me while I felt sick, while I grew round and while the baby stayed up all night. Seeing him hold a tiny new life that we had created together.

My heart stuttered. "I misspoke. Or rather, I meant children in general."

"Of course," he said.

"Lily could easily turn this room into a Pollock painting in ten minutes."

"I have no doubt. Although, I must tell you, this hideaway was not designed for children."

"I don't doubt it."

"It has always been the place where the Royals could escape to engage in fun. Obviously the house has been updated."

"Your parents came here together?"

"No. My father took lovers here. But I have had the house that he used razed to the ground. It has been under refurbishment for the past five years. This is the first time I have been here since."

"I find that all comforting."

"I thought you might. There is something quite distasteful about bringing your new bride into your father's former den of sin." His lip curled upward. "I find something distasteful about being in it myself. But as I said, none of that original structure remains."

His words seemed oddly symbolic, and I let them settle there for a while, but he didn't continue. Didn't elaborate on it all.

"So here we are, on our honeymoon," he said.

I shifted. "Yes. Here we are."

"You are welcome to change your mind about your rules."

Suddenly, my throat was dry. I felt parched, down to my soul, and he looked... Well, he looked like water. Like the only thing that might make me feel right.

"No," I said, stumbling backward. The moment brought to mind the story of Joseph in the Bible. When his master's wife had tried to seduce him, and he had run away, leaving his jacket behind.

I could imagine doing such a thing now. Running away and, if he grabbed hold of me, slipping out of my dress if I needed to.

But that only put me in mind of being naked with him, and that destroyed the point of the image in the first place. Which was to remind myself that sometimes the better part of valor was absolutely fleeing temptation.

"Then you will find your room at the end of the hall. Upstairs. You will not be bothered. It is perfectly fine for us to spend a week in solitude, I suppose."

"We don't have to be in solitude," I said.

He looked at me, and the expression in his eyes left the soles of my feet scorched. "Believe me," he said. "We do."

Isolation was easy in theory, but not so much in practice. My room was beautiful, my view of the beach, the white sand stretching out empty and pristine as far as my eye could see. And the ocean beyond might have kept me mesmerized for days on end, but I itched to be out in it.

The fact was, we were the only two people on the island, and even given all the space, we couldn't seem to stay away from each other.

Not quite.

We would pass each other on the stairs, down in the kitchen. The kitchen was the worst. Because there was something so unaccountably domestic about those familiar, everyday movements in a kitchen.

The opening and shutting of drawers, the clanging of

silverware, and there was no way that familiarity and domesticity should be attached to a king, especially not a king like Hercules, and yet it was even more impacting than those moments when I had stood in awe of him and his power.

He was a human. He drank coffee.

He walked around in bare feet.

And I was fascinated by him even more than when he had been a man of my fantasies. Something immortal and untouchable. A god from Mount Olympus.

I was fascinated by the way he ate fruit in the morning, by the way he took his coffee.

But I was also afraid to let him know that.

I would look at him out of the corner of my eye and then I would scurry back to safety, to isolation.

I would call Lily and then take a walk on the beach.

On the third day, he found me down there, by the water.

"You do love the beach, don't you?"

"I didn't know anything else for years. And it was always where I would go to be by myself."

"Until you met me."

I took a breath to say something to set him back, but…it left me. Because he was right. Until him. Solitude had been my escape, and then I had met him down by the water, and he had become my escape instead.

"All right. Until you."

"Tell me about Medland. Living on it."

"Why?"

He looked at me as though he was helpless to come up with the answer. "You're the mother of my child, and while we talked about a great many things, we avoided personal details. Someday it might come up in an interview."

But I didn't believe the answer.

"So quiet when no one was around. The people on the islands year-round don't have stacks of money. Or status. It's almost like a place set forty years back in time. Until the seasonal people come. And you know Medland is a high-end escape, for royalty such as yourself. Politicians. Actors. It moves from being the sleepiest, most down-to-earth little community you could possibly imagine into a strange collection of the world's elite, if only for a couple of months at a time. It was a wonderful and strange place to grow up. And being my father's daughter was... Well, I was homeschooled. I didn't attend school with any of the other kids. And no one would have wanted to be my friend anyway, because... Well, no one wanted my father getting wind of anyone's sins."

"I did whatever I wanted," he said. "Always. My father didn't care about debauchery, but he did care that I was strong. He wanted to turn me into a weapon. Strong for him and...callous, I think. And he wanted me to be like him. To care about the quest for power more than anything else, to consolidate our bloodline. To make us richer while the people continued to get poorer. But that is not me. I knew at a young age that I had to defeat him. Not join him."

"I don't know very many boys who would have come to that conclusion on their own."

"Surely it can't be that uncommon."

"I had to meet you to know that I could make another choice. That you discovered that on your own is... Well, it's truly wonderful."

I wanted to close the distance between us, because it felt right, out here on the sand with the ocean bearing witness, because it was something we'd done any number of times before. But not now. Not in this part of the lifetime.

"How did he try to make you tough?" I almost didn't want to know, but I felt that I had to ask. I was so curious about this man. This man that I'd only gotten a piece of all those years ago. But it had felt like everything to me. Only now was I realizing that physical nudity just scratched the surface of intimacy.

And did I really want to court intimacy with him? After all my talk of keeping things simple between us...

It wasn't sex. It was just talking.

"It doesn't matter," he said.

"Yes," I said. "It does."

"No," he said, his tone decisive. "It doesn't matter. Leave it alone."

And then he turned and left me alone, which was what I had said that I wanted.

And now I found I bitterly regretted it.

CHAPTER TEN

Hercules

SHE WAS TEMPTATION. Temptation in a way I was not in-
ured to. In truth, I had never much tested myself when
it came to resisting what I might want.

My childhood had been a harsh landscape. My father had taught me to withstand torture. Starvation.
Isolation.

And then he had told me that as a man I was free
to indulge my appetites as long as I knew how to go
without them.

It was a strange life. A firm, iron hand, combined
with no discipline at all.

I knew how to go without certain things. Affection,
food, water.

Apparently, I did not know how to go without Marissa when she was near.

She fascinated me. And I could tell that I fascinated
her. When she approached me, it was often with the
trepidation of a small mouse approaching a predator.
Her hands were often clasped, just below her chest,
her eyes bright as she would speak to me about some-

thing she liked—the food, the view, the way that the sun painted the sea with gold before it sank behind the horizon—and then she would scamper off as if she was afraid I might pounce on her at any moment.

She was not entirely wrong to be afraid.

I could not understand the point of resisting the thing between us, and yet she seemed to find it a moral necessity.

Except... I did understand. Why would she take a chance on a man like me?

I was not in the habit of talking to myself, but that had been happening more and more lately. As I questioned her, only to end up questioning myself.

All was running smoothly back in Pelion, at least as it had been reported to me. I received calls every day letting me know of the state of the nation. And I would take any necessary action that was required before going out of my office and into the rest of the house.

Going to Marissa.

To torture.

In many ways, Marissa was the perfect realization of what my father had raised me to endure. Indulgence and torture all rolled into one.

For I looked at her, and I was filled with desire, filled with lust, and I wanted her more than I had ever wanted anyone or anything.

And I constantly made sure that I was in her orbit, just to test my resolve. To test my strength. I wanted her.

I could not figure out why. I had never been able to.

It always came back to the way she had looked at me.

To the fact she wanted to talk to me. Didn't assume she knew what I thought about anything, but rather asked with an openness and innocence that shocked me.

I was distracted, thinking about Marissa when I should be thinking of the tasks ahead of me for the day, when the phone rang.

I answered, and the revelation on the other line turned the blood in my veins to ice as surely as Marissa turned it molten.

"Your father is dead." The palace official went on to tell me that my father had been found dead of an apparent suicide.

I could not fathom it. My father, the most self-interested man in the entire world, had ended his own life. He had never been anything but a master of his own self-preservation.

But then it suddenly made sense to me as I sat there in my office, my head reeling in darkness even as the sun rose high over the ocean.

He had chosen how it ended.

He had chosen it in a way that would make things the hardest for me. Because he knew that it would leave me with guilt, and if he left me with guilt, then how could I go on to sabotage his entire reputation? It was his final manipulation.

His final bit of torture. Rage tore me up inside as I tried to put the thoughts in my head in order.

Should I feel grief? Because he was dead, and there was no coming back from it. His revenge was hollow whether or not that was his intent.

Anger?

I did not want to bargain. Unless…

If I could only have had a few more words with him.
He would never know now. He thought he had won.

He would never see that he was the one in the wrong.

Because I could not believe that he had taken his
own life in a moment of despair. No. My father didn't
have it in him to feel despair.

He would never see. Now he never would.

There was something so desperately hollow in that.
Something appalling and vastly terrible in its scope.

Suddenly, I couldn't breathe. It reminded me of when
I had been a boy and he had put me inside of a box.
The kind of training that the military went through, he
had told me. And the leader of Pelion could not afford
to be any less stalwart than the military that protected
it, because they would go for the King first. My father
had told me that.

Isolation for hours, trapped inside of a box where I
couldn't even stand up.

That was how I felt now. Unable to breathe. Unable
to move. And I had to get out, because the walls of my
office were closing in around me in spite of the fact that
there were windows on all sides.

I did not know this feeling. I did not know helplessness. I did not know weakness.

Those things had been banished from me when I was
a boy. Banished at the hand of the man who put me in
that state now, and I hated him. Never had I hated him
more in life than I did now in death.

I stormed downstairs, the blackness inside of me an
entity that was beginning to escape. It had always been
there. It was not new. I knew that. I had always known
it was there. But I had always kept it locked behind a

wall. Only allowing glimpses out. Reminded when I walked through the obsidian halls of the palace and had it reflected back at me.

But I did not let it out.

But now it was as a torrent of living water. Destroying all that might come into its path.

But I was on an island where there were so few other souls.

But there was one.

And I knew... I knew that if she came near me now I would only destroy her.

I stumbled out of the house, down the path that led to the beach. And she was there. I had gone to find her. I had gone to find her because I no longer had it in me to fight. Not myself, not the beast inside of me and not the desire that I felt for her. Why had I resisted? All this time, why had I resisted?

Why had I allowed her these proclamations?

I was the King.

I was her husband.

She looked up at me, the wind whipping her dark hair around, those eyes bright as that little creature I had only just imagined her to be.

"We are through playing games." I stopped with just a foot between us. "I want you. Do not deny me."

"What has happened to you?"

But any words she might have intended to say next I cut off. I pulled her up against my body, and a muffled squeak rose from her mouth.

"You're mine," I said. "You have been mine for eight years. Since that first moment that I saw you on the beach. Do you not understand that every woman I took into my bed after you was a paltry imitation? Do you not understand that you took me and you turned me into a creature of longing, when I have never had to want for anything in my entire life? If I demanded it, it was mine. But not you. You ran from me. No one runs from me."

And I remembered her questioning that proclamation I had made when we had first reunited. I remembered her asking me if that was true.

And I pushed away the disquiet in my soul. I pushed away the answer.

And I held on to the lie.

And I held on to her.

"There you are," she whispered. And she did not look at me like she was terrified. Those bright eyes examined me, and she lifted her hand, brushing her fingertips against my mouth. "I've seen you like this before."

"You have not," I said. "You don't know who I am. No one does."

"I do," she said. "I saw it. That first day. It might not have been this close to the surface, but I saw it. You hide it from the world. You hide from yourself, but it's there, Hercules. I know it is."

"Is it why you ran away from me?"

"No. I ran away from you that first time because of how badly I wanted to run to you. And I was taught. I knew better. To want something the way that I want you... To feel that sickness inside of me... It could only be wickedness on my part, and so I ran from temptation. And I have run from temptation. Every moment since you have been back in my company, but it was not to please my father, and it was not to save my soul. It was just to save... I am in your world. There must be something of mine that remains."

"I need you," I said. And it galled me to say it. It was why I did not press the issue before, because I had been unwilling to show her how much I needed her. Unwilling to show her what her denial of her body to me cost me.

But I had no pride left.

My father was dead, and for the first time in my life, I had no idea what to do.

And I had run to her.

I was not a man who ran, and yet I had.

But not away from anything.

Just to her.

And I wondered if she would deny me, or if she would demand conversation first.

But instead, she stretched up on her toes and pressed her mouth to mine.

Marissa

He was falling apart inside, and I could see it. And I knew that there was every chance that touching him would pull me into the darkness right along with him. That I would not be able to protect myself once I'd allowed myself to be stripped bare with him. Especially when he was like this.

But this—as little as it made sense—was the part of him that I had always craved. And it was the part of him I had always been denied.

He had been the smooth playboy around me. He had

found something a little bit deeper, and a little bit more authentic, conversations with me that weren't about trading innuendo, but were about the things that we believed in our hearts.

But he had not shown me this.

I had witnessed it, like a voyeur staring through a window, that first time I had seen him when he had thought that no one was watching.

And that was what had ensnared me. I realized the truth of it now.

The whole truth.

For I had not known who he was.

It was not his wealth, his title, his reputation that had fascinated.

It was not the way he teased me. Not the way he laughed. Not the way he touched me or made me call his name.

It was knowing that there was more to him. That he had shown me something just a little more than he had shown anyone else. And that there was yet another secret I might reach.

And he was giving it to me now.

I didn't know why. And in the moment, I didn't want to ask. I didn't feel that I should.

Because he didn't want me to know. And if I asked him now it would break the spell. He might be able to gain his composure. And I did not want that. I wanted him like this.

And later, much later, perhaps I would ask myself where my sense of preservation had gone.

But I already knew the answer.

It went where it always had when it came to Hercules.

And here on this island, we were man and wife. King and Queen of each other and nothing more.

Lily wasn't here.

Here on this island, we were not parents who had been thrown together by our compatible fertility. We were not essential strangers who'd had to marry for a bloodline, for the throne.

We were not those who had taken vows in front of the church only days ago, to each other, to a nation.

We were just Hercules and Marissa.

Even our names seemed at odds, mine so typical.

His, that of a god.

But in this moment my god had fallen, and he needed me to hold him. He needed me to be there for him. To bear witness to this brokenness.

I would ask later why.

Later, we would talk.

But now…

Now I wanted only this. Only him.

I was not a saint, and I had given up the idea that I might be long ago.

In his arms, I was just a woman. And I needed him to satisfy me as only a man could. "If you want me, then take me," I said.

"Give yourself," he said, his voice rough. "Give yourself to me because you have to be in this. All of you. Because if you are not I might hurt you. I might do something you don't like. I need to know that this is not me taking with my darkness but you giving in to it. Step into it, Marissa, but do so of your own free will, because I do not trust myself. Not now."

Perhaps that should scare me.

But nothing about him had ever scared me. Not really. It had been my own self that I was always the most afraid of. The feelings that he called up inside of me, and the way that he made me act in a way that I thought was out of character. A way that I had discovered was my character, at least with him.

He had put me in touch with places and pieces and feelings inside of myself that I had not known existed. And he had made me like them.

Then he had taken himself away from me, and I had been left sitting in charred ruin. Not knowing what to do with this new version of myself, unable to go back to who I had been, unwilling to.

And cut off from the joy that I had found in being new at the same time.

He had taken my journey of discovery and made it a hard climb.

And yes, there was joy in being at the summit, joy in holding my daughter in my arms. Joy in who I had become after that long, hard slog.

But I wanted to return to that spark of joy.

I wanted to go back in time to the first moment I'd seen him and be woman enough to handle the bleakness that I had seen there.

But the good news was I could handle it now.

I had been given a gift. A gift of time. A gift of being able to be with him in the way that we both needed.

Desperately.

And so I did as he asked. So I stepped in with both feet.

I pressed my hands to his face and stretched up on my toes, and I claimed his mouth.

Doing that was exhilarating. Being the one to lean in. To take responsibility for all that we were, rather than being the helpless, innocent virgin. The seducer rather than the seduced.

Oh, I knew enough to know that we were both, he and I, wrapped up in this thing that we could not control. That we didn't want to—not anymore.

A bubble of laughter rose up in my throat, even as I kissed him.

"Something is funny?" he asked, his voice rough, and I knew that I was on dangerous ground.

"It's not really funny," I said. I pressed my hand to his chest. "I always imagined parents as some other *thing*. Off in the distance, remote and mature, and in possession of every answer to the universe. In my father's case, I imagined that he was basically omniscient. And here we are. Parents. And yet the same as we ever were. Still…with this. Between us."

"Because children make the mistake of believing that parents are something different entirely," he said, something dangerous and sharp on the edge of his voice. "That they are not human. When, in fact, that is all they are. And as fallible as any other."

"Yes," I agreed. "Yes." But I didn't say anything more. I simply kissed him again, my lips on his, moving, desperate for access so that I could go deeper. So that we could be consumed in this.

And he gave in, growling and wrapping his arms around me, folding me into the strength of his embrace. I had never felt so safe, so protected and yet so perilously close to danger as I did in that moment.

This was not the sweet touch of a man having deference for his much younger, less experienced lover.

This was a desperation between equals.

And nothing had ever made me more certain of the fact that this had to happen than realizing that.

That this King was standing with me, not above me.

I stripped his T-shirt from his body, marveling at all that golden skin. At the way the years had only improved him. Made his chest deeper, his waist slimmer and more defined. He had more hair on his body, and I found that I liked it. The touch of it. The way that it reminded me he was a man, and so very different from me.

He pulled my dress away, leaving me standing there in nothing but the brief bathing suit that had been provided for me on the island. But I wasn't embarrassed. Then he stood and began to examine me, and suddenly each and every difference in my body felt large and highlighted to me.

My curves were fuller, my stomach softer. White lines marred the place beneath my belly button and my thighs.

I'd had his child, and I bore the evidence of that.

And I wondered what he would say. What he would think.

There was nothing but that endless black fire in his eyes, and he said nothing. Then he reached behind me and untied the top on my bikini, sending it to the sand. He knelt before me and undid the ties on the bottoms. He looked up at me and I was engulfed in the black fire. But I didn't burn away. No, if anything, I only became stronger.

He leaned in, and he pressed his mouth to my stomach. Right to the spot where my skin had stretched, where it was looser now and nothing like how it had been the first time he'd been with me.

I closed my eyes tight, fighting back against tears. I didn't want to cry. I wanted to seize this moment with both hands, to dive into the debauchery of it. To be consumed in the intensity. I wanted to have this. With no thought for the future. No thought for consequences.

For the first time in my life, that was what I wanted.

But I couldn't banish the feeling. The deep, heavy emotion that wound itself around my heart, around my soul.

Because this wasn't just sex, and he wasn't just a man.

And we might not primarily be parents here on this island, but we made a life together.

And there was a heaviness to what we were.

Marissa and Hercules.

We couldn't erase the history between us. And in that moment I didn't even want to. Because it made it all that much more.

The weight was a blessing. The weight was a curse.

The tears spoke of the beauty as much as the sadness, and I wanted to embrace both.

And he was embracing me. The changes in my body. He took a tour of the map that spoke of the years we'd been apart. Of those nine months when I'd carried his daughter inside me.

He kissed every single one of those marks. His big hands explored my thighs, around to my bottom. And he ignited me.

More than just my skin, more than just desire, it was a feeling that was almost too big to be contained inside of my body.

An ache welled up between my legs, my breasts heavy, my nipples aching for his touch.

But if it had been only that, I could have walked away.

He had captured me somewhere deeper. Had made me want in a way that only he could satisfy.

And when I opened my eyes, when I looked at him again, the bleakness there terrified and compelled me.

Hercules.

My only lover. My only love.

My husband.

The list of all the things he was to me was long, and I wondered if it could ever be true for him.

Oh yes, I was his wife. The mother of his daughter.

But did that mean something to him? Did it mean anything beyond the legality?

It didn't matter. Not now.

Because now there were no barriers between us. Now he was taking his jeans off for me. Showing me that body that haunted my dreams.

His powerful thighs, his very powerful… The rest of him.

And when he came back to me, his naked body pressed against mine, he kissed me.

And every hot, hard inch of him was against every pliant, willing inch of me. It was right that it was here on the beach. Because it had always been the beach for us. Always the ocean.

As if we were ready to sail away at any moment, he and I.

But it had always been an illusion. There had always been a duty for him to return to, and there had always been reality to return to for me.

But not now.

Not now.

We were enfolded in his darkness, and I welcomed it. His hands were rough on my body, his whiskers a hard scrape against the tender skin of my breasts as he took my nipple into his mouth and sucked it deep.

The sharp sensation it created between my legs a glorious and honeyed pleasure that I craved. More.

More.

That was what my father had said about the road to ruin.

One step.

One step on the wide path.

The easy path.

You would keep going that way.

But nothing about this felt easy. It was hard in the most beautiful way. Too much and not enough all at the same time.

Heaven and hell converging on a beach.

As we had always been.

He slid his hands down my back, gripped my hips and pulled me up against him, urged me to stand on my toes, and then he lifted me up off of the sand by my thighs, wrapping my legs around his back as he took advantage of the fact that he now opened me to him. He braced me with one arm and put his hand between my legs, stroking me, stroking me until I cried out.

Until I thought I might cry.

He was brilliant. And we were brilliant together.

I had missed this.

As if a part of myself had been revived and I was now whole.

Then he laid me down on the sand, his hardness pressed against my center, and I arched against him, seeking to find the thing that I knew only he could give.

He had ruined even that for me.

Because the pursuit of my own pleasure, when I ached in the middle of the night and couldn't sleep, always took the shape of him.

He was a fantasy I could not banish.

I could want nothing and no one else.

So I had forgone even the pleasure of release on my own, because I couldn't bear to fantasize about the man who had abandoned me and my daughter.

But he hadn't.

And he was here. And he was mine.

And I was his.

"Give it to me," I whispered. "Give me your darkness."

And I did not have to ask him twice.

He wrapped his hand around my head, burying his fingers in my hair, lifting my head from the sand and kissing me with a punishing strength that took my breath away.

He shifted between my legs and surged inside of me, his strength, thickness and power causing me to gasp.

I was unused to this kind of penetration, and it hurt just a little bit.

And somehow that felt all right.

Somehow it felt fitting.

That this was like the first time.

He was in me. All around me.

We were one again, and that was the most right thing in the world even if I couldn't explain it. Even if I couldn't understand it.

His touch left trails of heat across my skin, and as he surged inside of me, over and over again, I was close to completion.

Not just in the sense of pleasure, but in the sense of a wholeness, a fullness and realness that I hadn't known had been absent from me.

The sun was behind his head, and each time he moved, a flash of light would blind my eyes and then it was him. Hercules.

And even when I closed my eyes, he filled my vision, the light from the sun painting ghosts behind my lids. Hercules.

It had always been him.

He had always been my sanity and insanity. My joy and my sadness. My ruin and my triumph.

He had always been.

He always would be.

And I realized in that moment, as I opened my eyes again and stared at that dear, beautiful face carved from rock, at those eyes that were capable of making me feel desired and making me feel destroyed. That mouth that I knew could deliver the most beautiful of compliments and the most cutting of cruelties, that this was what I had avoided.

Because I knew that once he touched me, it would be undeniable.

And I had thought that perhaps we could parent side by side and have some sort of sweet, amicable relationship. A marriage that was in a marriage. A life together that wasn't together. Hercules and Marissa with a space between them rather than wrapped around each other, but that had never been possible. And it never would be.

Because he was my other piece, whether or not I was ever his.

He had been the path to myself, and I had spent years living away from him, and I had not lost that.

My strength. The fortitude to stand on my own feet.

Even when I thought he had caused my diminishment, I had known that he had also created in me the strength to endure it.

The strength to go against my father, the confidence that what I felt and what I wanted was right.

A whole woman. Not a girl who was under the oppressive thumb of her father, who knew nothing of the real world or what she could be.

Hercules's woman. And that was when I shattered. Not slowly as he was doing, but one moment I was whole, come together completely, and then I was shattered, tossed into the wind like a billion stars in the sky.

And being broken with him was better than being whole had ever been.

Because he was the one who had made me.

And he was the one who had broken me.

I cried out his name as reality shattered through me, digging my fingernails into his shoulders. I had never done that before. I had never left a mark on him. But I would now. The joy that I took in our union would stay on his skin.

And I was proud of that.

With a growl, he froze, finding his own release that left him panting and spent just as I was, his forehead pressed against mine.

We shared the same air. Shared the same breath.

And for a moment we even seemed to share the same heartbeat.

But then that moment was over, and I remembered.

I remembered that he was bleeding something black and ugly from his soul, and I had managed to put a tourniquet on the wound, but I had not healed it.

I looked up at him, and I pressed my hand against his chest. "Tell me."

And on a ragged curse, still buried deep inside of me, he pressed his head against my neck and groaned. "My father is dead."

CHAPTER ELEVEN

Hercules

I DID NOT know what had possessed me to make that confession, still inside of her, still in reach of heaven.

I should not have done what I did. I should not have gone to her as I was. More beast than man, jagged and sharp and unable to control the rage that was coursing through me.

And Marissa did not deserve that.

Whatever I might have thought about her, she did not deserve that.

But she had said yes, and more than yes, she had taken the step toward me as I had demanded.

As if that had somehow taken the blame away from me. To put that squarely on her shoulders as I had done.

Take me.

She had commanded that I take her.

But she had taken me, and thoroughly at that.

In the sand, yet again.

Would I ever have this woman in a bed?

It was a question that I wanted an answer to.

But she had asked me a question, and it had nothing to do with when we might come together again.

I had answered.

And now there was a deathly, still silence between us.

She shifted beneath me. "I'm sorry," she said.

Two words. So quiet. Infused with sympathy.

Empathy.

She knew. She understood. That a horrible father could still be mourned, that the grief for someone such as him could be complicated and double-edged.

I barely understood it myself, but she did. Because she had been through it before. "It means it's over," she said softly. "And that is a terrible blessing."

Terrible blessing. A strange pairing of words, but she was right. It was a wholly terrible sort of blessing. To never have to deal with my father again, but also to never be able to experience the satisfaction of him being forced to change.

"For all I know," she said softly, "my father died believing that he did what's right where I was concerned."

I shifted, moving to lie beside her on the sand.

"Believing that ostracizing me, disowning his granddaughter… That it was the height of his piety. We never got to reconcile. Our final words were… Well, I didn't even speak. It was just him, telling me that I had to leave. Telling me it was the punishment for my sin. That Lily was a punishment. Perhaps it was something too large to repair. I don't know. But I would have very much liked for him to say he was sorry. To know that he knew he was wrong. Even if we could never have a relationship again, I would've wanted that."

"My father was a man beyond redemption," I said. "But I think I was waiting for that as well. For him to understand that he was the villain. But I believe that he died under the illusion that he was going to defeat me in his way. That he was the center of the story. And that he was the one who deserved triumph in the end. And that is…"

"It's not a good story," she said. "It's a terrible story. No one would want to read it, unless they were looking to feel sort of self-important. Unless they were looking to marinate in the gray areas of life, in which case I can only assume they don't have much experience with them. It's only a good story if it's not your reality. And for us…"

"It's uninteresting to watch them continue to be the heroes in their own worlds," I said.

"Very," she agreed.

"He was not a good man." I repeated it, mostly to myself.

She sat up, sand covering her bare body.

She looked so beautiful. She was different now, fuller breasts, fuller curves. She had a dusting of sand over her breasts, and I wanted to brush them off. And then put them in my hands. I was fascinated by her stretch marks. It made her pregnancy with Lily more real to me.

I wanted to focus on that, and not on the situation with my father. Not on the truth of him. Of my childhood.

But that darkness… I could not control it.

And everything was about to come spilling out.

"Do you know how elite military soldiers are trained?"

"No," Marissa said. "I can't say that I do."

She was clearly confused by the direction the conversation was going.

"In almost every country, a variant of these methods is used. But it is not just physical strength they must learn to withstand. They must learn to withstand physical torture. Because they are at risk for being tortured in order for the enemy to gain information. Torture is not simply shoving bamboo under people's fingernails. It is psychological as well. And the military in Pelion is well trained to withstand many forms of torture." I gritted my teeth. "My father believed that the ruler of Pelion must be trained to withstand it as well. He believed that I must be no less trained than our military. He started my training when I was a boy."

"When you were a boy?" She looked so horrified and I had regret that I was bringing my ugliness into her world. But we were the only people here. And she was the only one who had ever listened.

And for the first time in my life, I wanted to talk. Really talk. About what had created me. And what I really was.

"Yes. It was his belief that you created strength in a man early, or he would be compromised at the foundation. He approached me that way. As if I was something he was building. And I... I knew no different."

"Your mother..."

My heart felt like it was being squeezed. "Much like your mother, she did not have a say in most of her life."

She didn't try.

I clenched my jaw tight. There was no opposing the King. I'd had to go to great lengths in order to maneuver into a position where I might oppose my father. What hope would she have had?

Marissa looked away. "I think she would have put a stop to physically harming me."

"But you don't know. When powerful men with dangerous ideals ensnare those around them, when they feel powerless, what are they to do?"

I had repeated the same mantra to myself countless times over the years.

I ignored the hollow ache in my chest.

Like always.

"There were beatings, to be sure. Administered by some of his most elite soldiers. They knew how to make it hurt, but to avoid killing me. Very important, as killing me would defeat the purpose. But the beatings were easier to withstand than the other things. Being locked in a box with sound playing on a loop. Babies crying. Endlessly. I couldn't escape the noise. Sometimes they would strip me bare and hose me off with water as I lay on the cold ground. Shouting at me... Things I couldn't even understand.

"And they would demand that I denounce my father, and I would refuse. And that was how I won. Every time. That was how I proved my loyalty to the throne."

"Hercules..."

"No one has ever pitied me before," I said, marveling at her. "It is something of a novelty."

"Because everyone sees one piece of you. Everyone sees the money. Everyone sees the power, the money, the prestige. They don't know this."

"My upbringing was strict. Isolated. And then I was turned loose when I was fifteen. My father was confident that I had been trained, and he sent me out into the world and told me it was my buffet. I had the foundation I required."

"Why do you suppose he did that?"

"Truthfully? I think because he wanted to have it confirmed that his own debaucher nature was somehow ingrained in his blood. He wanted to watch me go out and do the very same. Have any woman that I pleased, buy expensive yachts and jets and go to the most exclusive parties and indulge myself in drinks and mood-altering substances. He wanted to believe that was the best a man could be, even when he was the very best man. He used me in a variety of ways, and that was just one of them. He created with me a perfect soldier—so he thought—and he created a mirror that showed him what he wanted. But inside I have always been different. I have always known that he was wrong. And when those men told me to denounce my father, I did it a thousand times inside. I didn't speak, not because I was afraid, but because I knew that my father could not see into my mind. Because I knew that I had to stage my coup in the neatest way possible. I feared, always, that any bad behavior would blow back on my mother, and later my sister."

"You feared for your mother's safety?" Marissa asked.

"Yes, of course."

"But she did not fear for yours. Or she was too afraid to act out and protect you. How can you worry for her?"

I shifted, and so did something in my chest. "She was not created to be strong. I was. I was not going to allow what he did to me to break me, Marissa. You must understand that. I had no control over it. No control over what happened to me. But I could allow it to forge me into the blade that would eventually kill my father. I didn't know that it would be quite so literal. I had imagined that it would be political in nature, and it very nearly was. I suspect… I suspect in essence he wanted me to feel that it was me who made that fatal blow."

"Because he knew that it would hurt you."

"Perhaps. Though, I think *hurt* is too strong a word. I'm not sure that he believes I possess the ability to be hurt. I'm not sure if I do either."

"You are hurt. I saw you when you came down from the house. This hurts you terribly."

I shook my head. "Animals feel pain. It's not the same."

"You think you're more like an animal?"

"Elemental. As I was trained to be. I do not feel far beyond what the basest creatures do. I do not have the ability."

"I think you do. I've watched you with Lily."

"It is beneficial for me to be kind to Lily."

I felt nothing when I spoke her name, and I was glad of it. I suddenly felt hollow, and I was glad of that as well.

"That's not the only reason," she said.

"Don't make the mistake of thinking that you know me," I said to her. But I was saying it to my own self as well. For it was easy to lie here with her in the sand, a moment out of time. Which was what we had always had. But when we returned, we would be returning to the palace, and I would be King. I could not afford to take that lightly, nor could I afford to assume that I knew everything about myself or what I was capable of.

I had been created by the hand of a monster, after all.

And the real danger was assuming that I could control the matching creature that lived inside myself.

That darkness.

She said nothing, but the way she looked at me clearly spoke the words for her.

She was intent on seeing the best in me. And I wondered if it was because she had consented to be mine again.

If she had to tell herself that on some level I was a good man or feel sullied by what had happened between us.

Marissa was a good woman.

Of that I was confident.

If anything had changed over the course of the week at the island, it was my certainty of that.

I had spent five years thinking of her as a defector. As one who had betrayed me in a way that no other woman had—because no other woman abandoning me would have felt like a betrayal.

But I had relearned her.

And perhaps the best thing was having confirmed that I had been right about one thing at least.

She was exceptional. She was like no one else. And that meant that I would have to be careful.

She was the one who would have to take the largest part in raising Lily. Because she was the one who would shape the best ruler, one who had not been touched by my father at all. I would make a conscious decision to correct what I could, but Lily would be unspoiled.

Of that, I was certain. Of that, I was resolved.

"Let us go back to the house," I said.

"Will we need to return for your father's funeral?"

I leaned in, and I kissed her, fiercely. "That man has stolen enough from me. He will not steal this too."

That seemed to soothe her, and she leaned against me. Trust. She should trust in me, as did Lily.

I would do my utmost not to disappoint them.

But that would mean keeping my distance.

But we had until the end of this week.

And I would take that with both hands, and her as well.

For when we returned to Pelion, things would have to change.

CHAPTER TWELVE

Marissa

THE TIME ON the island slipped away too quickly. I was angry at myself for spending a week avoiding him, when we could have been together. I was blissfully happy, but I missed Lily.

Of course, when we left here, I would miss being with him as we were now. I knew that. I somehow sensed that things were going to change.

Of course they would.

We would be back in a world that was completely foreign to me. I didn't know how to be a queen.

I didn't know how to live in this country; I didn't know the customs; I didn't know the way of it. Much less how to be royalty within it.

And so, I decided to ask him.

I felt raw, wounded by our coming together down at the beach, but more than that, the conversation we had after.

Thinking of what his father had done to him...

It tore me to pieces inside.

To think that a parent could do such a thing to their child… It was beyond imagining.

And he seemed to think…that he was fine. But I could see that he was not.

Or if not fine, he seemed to think that whatever remained in him was for the best, something that made him the sort of opponent that his father had required.

When I looked at him, I saw a wounded boy. And I knew he would not like that. Not at all.

So I didn't say that to him. Instead, I would touch him whenever I could, not just to solidify the sexual connection, but to find closeness. To offer comfort. I found myself wondering if anyone had ever touched him kindly when he was a child.

Or if all he had known was abuse and negligence. In some ways, he was right. And my mother could easily be accused of actions similar to his own. She had certainly been unable to act against my father in a meaningful way in those years when I had been banished from the home.

But I had read about his mother. About all the traveling she did, the way that she flitted off to tropical islands at her leisure. The rumors that the young Princess was not the daughter of the King.

And I did not doubt that Hercules had believed he needed to protect them. I could see it in the way that he spoke. In every line of his body. He was protective of them.

And from what I had heard about his father, possibly rightly so.

But I had a suspicion that his father more or less

ignored his wife and daughter, and did as he pleased with other women, and did as he saw fit to Hercules.

I wondered how much of the threat directed at Hercules's mother and sister was simply a smoke screen set up by his father. A way to take advantage of the good nature that his son had. Because of course the King possessed none of his own.

I knew that Hercules mourned him in a strange way. But I would not mourn King Xerxes. Not for a moment. Not after the way I had learned he had harmed Hercules.

The physical scars might have long healed, but his emotional scars were deep.

I thought about Lily and the way he seemed afraid to connect with her. Though, he seemed to try at that more than he did anything else. He was a good man, of that I was convinced.

It wasn't that he was incapable of connecting with Lily, or that he didn't want to. To me it seemed as if he was truly frightened.

Of her, of something in himself, I didn't know.

I wanted to fix it.

But I knew that I couldn't.

So instead, I decided to give him a chance to fix me, because that might give him something to tether him to the earth.

"I don't know how to be a queen," I said to him over coffee the morning before our last here on the island.

"Come to think of it," he said, his tone dry, "I'm not sure there is a very decent precedent set for a queen in Pelion."

It was the first time I had ever heard him come remotely close to insulting his mother.

"In what way?"

"You may have noticed that my mother is absent from the country most of the time."

"Yes. Will she return for your father's funeral?"

"Oh, I suppose. They were still married, whether or not they had a relationship."

"And you are not concerned about the rumors that will come from you not going?"

"There will be rumors, of course. But I stand ready to repudiate nearly everything about my father's rule. I will lead with this. And I will make a statement."

I was struck by his strength. By the way his face seemed almost carved from granite.

He was truly an incredible man.

"You're not afraid of scandal, then," I said.

"The only reason that I cared about marrying a suitable woman was that was part of the rules set for my father's early abdication. Once I found out about Lily, I was able to institute a bit of blackmail to ask him to step aside. But then he did the most convenient thing I could imagine and died."

"Well," I said, laughing reluctantly at his dark comment. "I suppose."

"I have never cared anything for convention. For in my eyes, the conventions established in my country were little more than a joke. Ways to keep pompous men like my father in power."

"Has there ever been a queen? I mean…a queen like Lily."

"No," he said. "In fact, that makes me suspicious that they might have…" He grimaced. "I don't even want to think about it. Hopefully no one made a practice of eliminating heirs to the throne based on their gender. Though, they might have just made them go away, the way that he did with Lily."

"He didn't know her gender when he did that."

"No, indeed. But that had everything to do with keeping me from taking power any sooner than I might have." He shook his head. "No. I don't care one bit for the pomp and circumstance of the Xenakis family. We are making a new country. And so you will be the Queen that you decide to be."

"I'm just a girl from an island who happened to meet a prince."

"A prince with very poor self-control," he said.

"That's not true. I think you have amazing self-control, and any indication to the contrary is a little bit of a put-on."

"I didn't have self-control with you."

I took that and held it close to my chest. "Well, I suppose that makes me special."

"There is no *suppose* about it. You are unlike anyone else I have ever known."

The admission seemed uncomfortable for him. Seemed torn from him.

"Then I suppose I will keep aiming for that as Queen."

"Do you have any special interests?"

"The care of single mothers," I said instantly. "Believe me when I tell you we face an inordinate amount of judgment while the men often responsible walk around without any."

"Perfect," he said.

"Perfect?" I repeated.

"Not perfect that they face judgment. But perfect that

you have such a strong and clear interest. That will be your vocation, if you would like."

"I would," I said. "You know, I was so focused on taking care of Lily that I never truly thought about having work. Or…a calling, I suppose. I was given so much money by…well, your father…that I was able to buy a house, and we were able to live quite comfortably. When she was older, I would have had to find something to do, but that wasn't encouraged in my home either. Women working. Having aspirations. So I just didn't. But I like the idea of this."

"Being Queen can be a vocation. A calling. No one else has taken it that way for my country in the past, but you could be the first."

"I imagine I'd also be the first to marry the King after our child is born?"

"Likely. Unless, again, there has been some revision in the history books."

"Well, we can always assume there might be. I don't mind being the first. Just another way that we are an oddity. Just another way that we will help change the country. I mean, not to co-opt your revolution."

He laughed. "No, it's perfectly fine if you want to join the revolution with me. You're free to pick up a sword."

"I hadn't realized that swords would be part of the job description."

"I can get you one."

"I don't think that's necessary." Our eyes caught and held, and heat spiked between us.

What a strange and wonderful thing to have both, this ability to laugh with him and want him all at the same time.

"I have some things to see to," he said. "I will… I'll find you."

There was something deep in that. Enduring. A promise that echoed in my soul. At least, I chose to let it.

"Okay," I said.

I chose not to dwell on the end of our time here.

I had to start thinking of it as a beginning. No matter how difficult it was. When we returned to the palace, we settled into a pattern. But it was one I didn't expect. It was reminiscent of our first days on the island. Hercules avoided me. At least, that was what it felt like. Perhaps that wasn't what was happening.

He was wrapped up in affairs of state. I discovered quickly that life as royalty did not simply mean a life doing whatever you wanted.

Not that I didn't have a sense of that before—I had seen news stories about royals all my life, but it wasn't as if I had paid close attention to them, and I definitely hadn't considered it some kind of guide for my potential later life.

I had never imagined that I might become a queen.

But here I was.

I spent a few hours a day working on ideas for outreach to single mothers in the community. I looked at budgets and talked to palace officials about things like free day-care centers and maternity leave.

It was fulfilling work. And when I wasn't doing that, I was taking care of Lily. Lily made me happy too, as she always had.

It was nice, also, spending time with my mother. We had years spent apart, and we hadn't talked like we did in the palace in… Ever.

But I was still lonely. I missed Hercules. I missed wasting hours talking to him about everything and nothing. I missed sleeping with him at night.

We kept separate bedrooms here.

I didn't like it.

"What's wrong?" my mother asked one day as we sat in the garden of the palace, where a massive play structure had been erected for Lily. She was running around, her dark hair flying behind her as she ran, her laughter filling the staid silence of the royal grounds.

I loved that.

Especially knowing what I did about Hercules's childhood.

"Nothing," I said.

"That's a lie," my mother said. "I know you well enough to know that, even if I haven't known you as well as I should have for the past few years."

"You couldn't help any of that. There's no point in regret."

"I don't say this because I am experiencing regret. At least, not so much. But I can tell that you're not happy. When you came back from your honeymoon you seemed…different."

"Well, it's nice to be on a private island without any responsibilities."

"And now you have responsibilities."

"Good ones," I said. "But it is a lot."

"I don't think hard work has ever scared you, Marissa. Somehow, I don't think that's what's bothering you."

"It's… Hercules has been very busy."

"I've never known as much about the two of you as I should. I was forbidden from speaking about you when your father was still alive. And we never got a chance to…"

"I fell in love with him," I said. "The first time I ever saw him. I was sixteen. He didn't touch me then," I said hurriedly. "But we got to know each other. Every summer. More and more. And I… I didn't have the will-power to resist him."

My mother looked thoughtful. I didn't know what to expect from her. If she would judge me for that weakness or not.

"I was envious of you in some ways," my mother said. "I was never carried away by passion of any kind. I married sensibly. I married a man that my parents approved of. There was no joy in our marriage. And we couldn't speak. I could never tell your father what I wanted from life. I let him send my daughter away because I didn't have the fortitude to stand on my own two feet and speak for myself. I let you be badly treated because I didn't stand up for you. And I have regretted it every day since."

"There is room for regret between us," I said. "Mom, I know how Dad was. I don't blame you."

"Perhaps you should. I look at the way you protect Lily, how you've given everything to her, and I should have done the same for you."

"You weren't able to. I know that. I understand it."

"I wish… I wish I would have had a different life. I wish I would have stood up and said what I wanted."

"Do you really think that he would have given it to you?"

"He might have given me a divorce, and in the end, perhaps that would have been better."

"Maybe," I said.

But I didn't really think so. I don't know what my mother would have done. I was glad that she was coming into her own strength now, but she couldn't regret who she had been all those years. She couldn't change it.

And I didn't want her to make herself sick over it.

"I guess my point in bringing any of this up is that if you want something different with Hercules, then you should speak up. Otherwise you end up with a lifetime of regret and sadness. You look back and you wonder how you spent so many great years just enduring. Brittle silence and the full absence of a loving touch. I don't know how or why I subjected myself to that. And maybe I couldn't have had a different marriage with your father, but perhaps I could have had a different life. Perhaps you could have had a different life. But you still can. Don't build castles made of regret, because they're what you'll live in in the future. Believe me."

"What if he doesn't want different?"

Because that was the thing that really scared me.

"Then you'll be angry. And hurt. But you won't have to wonder. You won't have to wonder if there was something you could have done but were too afraid. Your relationship with Hercules…it's for Lily too. If you need that, then remember that as well. But if you could do it just for yourself… Marissa, that would be a very brave thing to do." She sighed. "To do more than just endure is a brave thing." My mother's words stayed with me for the rest of the day.

I did know how to endure. I had gotten very good at it. I had accepted a life where I wouldn't have love.

Where I wouldn't have Hercules. In many ways, I had accepted my fate as a martyr to the cause of my daughter, and that was what had made it so easy to go back with Hercules and use Lily as the sole excuse.

But that hope…

That hope inside of me meant something.

It was for me. It was for him. For us and for our love. For what could be.

I had seen the possibility of all that five years ago, and I could still see it now. I wanted it. I craved it.

But I was denying myself because I had looked into my father's icy stare and been sent away before. Because my mother hadn't stood up and told me to stay. Or that she would go with me.

Because I had felt abandoned, by my parents, by Hercules.

It had been so much easier to let go, to accept the fact that I walked through life alone, except for Lily. That I lived for her, that I breathed for her.

And there was nothing wrong with that. I did. She was my daughter, and it was my great joy to sacrifice for her.

But there was more. I wanted more.

And wanting more for myself meant wanting more for Lily.

I wanted her to have a happy home. And no, it would never be conventional, because we lived in a castle. There would always be staff around; there would always be matters of state to see to. But we would never want for anything. There were incredibly wonderful, privileged things we could have as well, but why couldn't we have love on top of that?

The house that I had grown up in had been stale.

My mother had been right. It had been gray.

And I had gone to escape the gray down at the shores of the ocean, where I had found Hercules.

He had been my escape. He had been my salvation, not my ruin.

But only if I was willing to reach out a hand and ask.

Ask to be saved. For both of our sakes.

Because we could have one of two lives. The gray and the bleak, or we could have it all.

We could have paradise. A walk through the fog, or a life staring out at the bright, brilliant sea.

And I knew which one I felt we were meant to have. I knew what I wanted. But one of us was going to have to be brave enough to take it.

I knew all that Hercules had been through, and I could understand why the inside of him felt a little bit too broken for things like love.

But I also knew that he could make a decision to put it behind him.

I also knew that we could have more, that bravery might have a cost, and love might take work, but it was worth it in the end.

For what Hercules and I could have was a jewel beyond price, and I had to be willing to sell everything I owned to possess it. All of it.

I had to be willing to do more than exist in the possibility of a relationship and throw down a definitive gauntlet.

Do you always do as you're told?

He had asked me that once, so long ago. And that was when I had realized that I did, and that I didn't want to, not anymore.

It was the same now.

I didn't want to simply do as was expected. I didn't want to do as I was told.

I wanted to live bright and brilliant, with him, with our hearts twined around each other as I knew they could be.

Not two separate people living two separate lives in a massive palace, but two souls that had become one.

He might not believe in that, but I did.

And that meant that I had to be the one to fight for it.

He wanted reason, and I didn't have reason.

But I had love.

Hercules had told me once that he believed in the physical. Well, I would approach him that way. I would give him what he understood before I introduced what he felt he could not. And maybe then those two things would come together for him and create something new.

Something that was only ours.

Something that he could see and touch and feel.

I was afraid.

Like I had been afraid that first time we'd been together down on the beach.

But I was also determined. And I knew what I wanted. I knew who I was.

I could only hope that Hercules would come to understand the same way that I did.

Because if he did...

If he did, then he wouldn't want to accept less either.

But there was no way for me to know. So I had to step out in faith.

I had to be brave.

CHAPTER THIRTEEN

Hercules

I HAD DONE my very best to throw myself into the leadership of Pelion. It was difficult when I was obsessed with erotic thoughts about my wife. I knew that she was unhappy. The few times that I had seen her since we had returned from the island, she had been a bit sullen with me. At dinner she had been quiet, and the air had been filled by chatter coming from Lily, and I knew that I had been disengaged with that as well.

But I had to rule. I had to be King. There was no scope for me to be distracted by my family.

My family.

Marissa and Lily were my family.

Such a strange and foreign concept to me.

I couldn't remember having family dinners when I was growing up. No, I ate in the nursery; my mother was usually away. By the time my sister was born, I was nearly grown.

I didn't remember saying that we could have family dinners, but one evening Marissa, her mother and Lily showed up and sat at the table. The staff brought dinner to all of us, and so it had continued on every night since.

But even as we had those dinners, and Marissa would respond to the things I said with brightness, I could sense that beneath it she was unhappy.

I didn't like that, but I didn't know what else she wanted from me either.

I was the leader of a nation. I had concerns I had to put above all else. Including the two of us.

From everything I'd been told by my staff, Marissa was adapting beautifully to her role as Queen. And yet...

She was different than she had been on our honeymoon.

But then, so was I. Of necessity. I had allowed myself to be distracted by her there. I had broken there. I had shown weakness, and that could not be allowed. If my father had died, and I had not had a soft spot to land in the form of Marissa's arms, how would it have gone?

Instead, I had splintered, and I had allowed my darkness to pour out, to spill onto my wife, and that was unacceptable.

I knew that.

And so, we would continue to be separate. We would continue to have separate rooms. Until such time as I felt that I had a grip on...everything. From the running of the palace to my emotions.

My emotions. The fact that I had them at all made me feel weak.

I despised it.

Even in the form of rage I was beginning to find them unwieldy.

I disliked it.

It made me wonder if I was closer to my father than I had ever anticipated.

I liked to pretend that I was something else. Something different entirely, but I wondered.

Was there any way to fully escape being like your maker when he had fashioned you in his image? It was not something I knew the answer to, and I feared that only time would tell.

But in the meantime, I would not affect Marissa and Lily.

It was the one good thing I knew I could do. Keep my distance.

I had been spending every night in my office, staying up as late as I possibly could to ensure that I fell into bed in exhaustion that would prevent me from going down the hall and taking Marissa again and again.

She was a temptation that I was finding difficult to resist, and that was yet more reason to resist her.

I couldn't allow her to have control over me.

I couldn't allow anyone or anything to have control over me. Not my base desires, not my lust and certainly not my wife.

Those things made for a weak king, and I refused to be weak. Had I not spent my childhood trying to demonstrate my strength? I would not falter now.

My father was wrong. You did not have to be a monster to rule. I would show that until my dying day.

But in order to do that, I had to make sure that I did not falter.

When work didn't help, I went to the gym. And I exhausted myself there. Tonight, thankfully, I was exhausted without punishing my body, and when the time was past midnight, I finally went to my quarters.

The palace was quiet, dark and empty, the obsidian halls glittering bleakly in the blackness.

It felt all too close to what was going on inside of me.

I pushed the door open to my chambers, and the lights were on.

The flood of brightness was a shock after walking down the long, dark hall.

But not as much of a shock as the sight that greeted me.

Marissa, lying on the bed, completely naked.

She did not look defeated now. She did not look shy or innocent. She was bold. There was nothing on her body, and she reclined across the pillows in a way that emphasized her curves. The glorious plumpness of her breasts, the indent of her waist, the round swell of her hips.

And those nipples... Dusky berry and tight, begging for my attention. That dark thatch of curls between her thighs that I wanted to bury my face in.

I had spent days resisting this very thing, and now I wasn't certain I had it in me to resist any longer.

"What are you doing here?"

She moved her hand, and the only thing that adorned her body—our ring—glimmered there.

"I missed you," she said softly.

They were not the words of the siren, and they were not the words that I had expected. They were emotional, spoken with a sweetness that truly stunned me.

"Did you?" I asked.

"Yes," she said softly.

"You could have simply told me over dinner."

"I don't want to talk," she said.

The words were a male fantasy, and not ones I could quite credit coming out of Marissa's mouth. Because if there was one thing we had always done, it was talk. Even when passion was hot between us, we always spoke.

"You don't want to talk?"

"No," she said, shaking her head, her glossy mane shimmering in the light. "I can talk to anyone. You're the only man that I can do this with. The only man I've ever been with at all. The only man I will ever be with."

Something twisted hard and low in my stomach. "The only man you've ever been with?"

"Did you imagine that I was entertaining lovers these last few years?"

"You would have been forgiven for doing so. You are human, after all. And humans have needs."

"But you ruined me for everyone else."

"You see," I said darkly, "you ruined me for everyone else as well, but that did not stop me from…" I began to remove my shirt, and I questioned my own resolve and strength the entire time. Still, it didn't prevent me from doing it. "That made it all the worse. It was hollow. The promise of a feast, but when I reached out to take it in hand, it just turned to ash. Bitterness in my mouth. It was never what I wanted. Because I had tasted…paradise. I tasted paradise on your skin, Marissa, and then it was gone. I knew what making love could be, and it was never that, not after you."

"Well, I was just smart enough to know that I didn't want to substitute."

I felt humbled by that. Because I hadn't been. I had been angry and filled with thwarted pride, and I had tried to erase her from my body, from my skin, in the beds of other women. I didn't like the way that made me feel. I didn't like the shame. Didn't like the heavy, hot emotion that stabbed me in the chest and seemed to twist my heart into strange and unnatural shapes.

She was twisting me into strange and unnatural shapes inside, and I didn't know what the hell I was supposed to do about it. I was supposed to be supreme and sovereign ruler, or something like that, and yet... And yet.

I shoved my trousers off, left them down on the ground, and the rest of my clothes along with them.

I was past the point of pretending that I was going to resist.

It was one thing to keep separate when she was across the palace, but it was quite another when she was naked and in my bed.

I had to ask myself who this man was that he couldn't control himself around a woman. Ever.

That she had been my downfall there on the island, and I had learned nothing in the time since.

But she said she didn't want to talk, and she said she only wanted me, and why couldn't I take her like I did any other woman? She was still paradise, still Marissa, and I should be able to have whatever sort of physical relationship with her that I desired. It would feel the same.

I'd had any number of emotionless sexual experiences, and there was no reason she couldn't be the same. She would have to be. If we were going to continue, if this were going to continue, then we would have to.

And I couldn't live with her, not in the same sphere and resist her. So we would have to.

She moved, getting up on her knees and sliding her hand slowly across my chest. She was angling to kiss my mouth and I grabbed her chin, stopping her. "No."

"Why not?"

"You said you didn't want to talk," I said. "So don't talk."

A fire lit behind her eyes, but she didn't speak.

I pinched her chin between my thumb and forefinger and guided her slowly downward. She knew what I wanted.

She parted her lips, the expression in her eyes bright. And then she dragged her tongue along the head of my arousal, and I let my head fall back, luxuriating in the soft, slick pleasure as she took me deep into her mouth, making low, satisfied sounds as she did.

We hadn't had the time to play at such things when we'd been younger, desperate to couple together out in the open, and with no time for extras in case we might get caught.

I had thought about this, though. With her. So many times that I'd lost count.

She had no experience, and I could see that, but what she didn't have in experience she made up for with her very clear desire for it. For me.

She wasn't timid; she wasn't uncertain. She took me in deep, wrapping her hand around the base of me and tasting me slowly and thoroughly.

It was heaven and hell, all contained in this woman. It always had been.

She lowered her head, her dark hair falling over her

face, and I tried to force myself to pretend that she was just one of the substitutes that I'd had in the years between our coming together again.

That she didn't matter.

That she was no one.

But I couldn't, and I didn't want to. Because the minute that I tried to imagine it was anyone other than Marissa, the spark was gone. She mattered.

I gritted my teeth. I arched my hips upward, and she accepted me, took me in deeper.

I was getting close to the edge, unable to hold myself back any longer, and I guided her away. She made a soft sound of protest, but I wouldn't hear of it.

"That isn't how this is going to end," I said. "On your knees."

She looked at me. "I already am."

"Turn around," I said, and she obeyed.

I looked at her, the long line of her elegant back, moving down to the full curves of her ass. Her glossy hair was draped over her shoulder, exposing all that skin. And she was exquisite. More than beautiful.

Desire coursed through me, hot and hard as I approached her. I put my hands on her shoulders, slid them down her back, around to grip her hips hard, watching as my fingers left impressions in her skin. Then I reached between her legs and stroked her until her wetness coated my fingers, until her desire was all over my skin. She whimpered, gasping as I pushed two fingers inside of her, rocking her hips back and begging.

I had control. She might have come in here to seduce me, might have come in here to prove some kind of point, but the point would be mine in the end.

I would have her, however I wanted, whenever I wanted, and she would allow it, because she was mine.

Maybe I couldn't pretend that she was someone else. Maybe I couldn't make it carry less weight, but I could stay in control of this.

I commanded; she obeyed.

That could work.

We could work.

Because God knew I couldn't stay away.

She made a little kittenish cry, arching back, the motion pushing my fingers deeper into her body, and my arousal pulsed with need. I pulled away from her, positioning myself at the entrance to her body, teasing her, sliding my length through her folds before moving back to her opening and pushing in just slightly, before repeating the motion again.

She was panting, near to crying, when I finally gave her what we both wanted.

I gripped her hips hard and pushed in, rough and deep.

But she didn't seem to mind.

No, if her cry of pleasure was any indicator, she was more than happy with my desperation.

And that meant that I would have hers.

Because this could not be a meeting of equals. I had to make sure that she was the one who was desperate. She was the one who was reduced. Because I could not afford to be.

I pumped into her, chasing my release, chasing our end. She whimpered, and I pressed my hand between her shoulder blades, pushing her chest down flat on the bed, keeping her hips raised up. Then I grabbed hold of her arms, wrapped my hand around her wrist and pinned it to her lower back, then the other. I held her tight as I thrust into her, over and over again, the angle letting me go deep, the way I had her pinned keeping her motionless.

"Please," she whimpered, "please."

But I refused to end it. I kept it going, torturing her, torturing myself, the bright, brilliant flashes of pleasure that consumed me a torment that I didn't want to end. I knew what she needed. I knew that she needed me to touch her between her legs so that she could come. Or that she needed to touch herself, but I had her captive.

She began to shake, she began to weep, and I moved harder inside of her, until we had slid up the mattress, until I had to brace myself on the headboard, so we didn't collide into it. I freed her hands when I did, and she used the opportunity to shift, wiggling and putting her hands between her legs as I continued to pump inside of her.

"Don't," I bit out. "Not until I say."

"I need to," she said.

"You are my wife," I said. "My Queen. Your body belongs to me."

She went still. "Yes," she whispered. "But your body belongs to me."

She reached between her legs, beneath us, and stroked me at the point where our bodies met, and I shuddered, cursing as she did so.

"Witch," I said, finally agreeing to give her what she wanted.

I put my hand where I knew she needed me, and I pinched her gently, before stroking her, keeping time with my thrusts.

And then there were no games, no more fights for

control, because there was only pleasure. Wrapping around us, binding us together.

And when we both found our release, it was together, the violence of it shaking us, shaking the bed, shaking the very stone the palace was made of.

Shaking what I was made of.

And when it had ended, she curled up against my chest, and I couldn't play games any longer.

I hadn't won anything. I hadn't distanced myself.

When her fingers traced delicate shapes over my chest, I couldn't pretend she wasn't Marissa, couldn't pretend that it would ever be anything but heavy.

"Hercules," she whispered, "I love you."

Marissa

And that was when the walls fell down around us. My heart was still beating hard from my release. But more than that. From the admission that had just fallen from my lips. I wasn't afraid, though. There was no place for fear here. Inside my body. How could I fear when I was in his arms?

Hercules was my husband, the father of my daughter. He was the man that I loved. And with him I had always felt an absence of fear. With him I had always felt strong and solid in who I was. And what I knew from talking to my mother was this: what you allow will continue.

And I could allow for us to continue on in unspoken words. I could allow for us to stay in a world where I let safety mean more than truth.

But I didn't want that. And I didn't have to allow it.

"I love you," I repeated, again.

He shifted. "No," he said, simply, definitively.

"Hercules, I don't know who you think you're speaking to, but I am neither your daughter nor one of your subjects. I am your wife. And you don't get to tell me *no* as a response to *I love you*."

"I... No. I cannot accept."

"It wasn't a gift. It was a statement of fact."

On some level, I wasn't surprised at his denial. On some level, this didn't shock or wound me. Because how could it? This was who he was. A man made of rock, and for some reason he seemed to need to cling to the facade.

I knew that I would have to break the walls down. I knew that I couldn't simply walk up to the door and ask for entry. No. I had asked for entry, and now I would have to be willing to do battle.

"You don't understand. There is no room in my life for these kinds of emotions."

"Why not? What about Lily?"

"This has nothing to do with Lily."

"Do you love her?"

"But that is a foolish question. I have known her for a matter of weeks."

"She's your daughter. That's... That's not how that works. I've loved Lily from the moment she first came into the world, and I can tell you I didn't know her then. With children, it's not a matter of knowing them, is it? It's a matter of knowing that their lives are in your hands. That you must protect them, that you must care for them. That without you they won't know anything of the world. You're meant to be her conscience, her guidance. Her place of protection. And that... Let me tell you, Hercules, that produces feelings of love faster than knowing someone ever could. So do you intend to never love your daughter? Because you will be the only father that she ever has."

"I didn't need love. I didn't need love—it was weak, and it did nothing."

"Your father didn't love you. At least, not in the way that a normal person should. He didn't demonstrate love."

And then Hercules exploded. "Not my father. My mother. My father never said that he loved me. My father never lowered himself to tell such a lie. He never would. It was her. *I love you.* She would whisper that. Over my bruised body, but she would never do anything to stop it."

"Hercules…"

"She couldn't, and I understand that, but what did her love get for me? It meant nothing. She would go off, because she claimed she couldn't stand to see the way that he treated me, but she left me here with him. She had another child for the sole purpose of having one that she could…that she could love in the way that she wanted. Because she had to surrender me to him. So, you tell me what love ever did for me. You tell me how love makes a family. Because it never did in mine."

"Hercules," I said softly. "Your mother was wrong. Your father was wrong."

"That's a lot of people who were supposed to love me being wrong, Marissa. At a certain point a man must acknowledge that the problem might be with him."

"I love you. You think I would allow you to be submitted to torture? Do you think I wouldn't die for you?"

"No," he said, the admission ferocious. "Never offer such a thing to me. I don't deserve it. I am not worth that. Don't you ever say something like that to me again."

"Why must you reject it so?"

"Because I am last—do you understand me? That is how I must see myself. My father saw himself as first. Above all else, above anything, sovereign to the entire world. And look at the things he did. To me. To my mother."

"Hercules, your parents were broken. Undeniably. I am sorry if your mother had a difficult time of it, but that doesn't give her an excuse to allow her child to be abused. She had money. She could've fled with you. The UN would have taken care of you, something. There must have been a way that you could have escaped."

"It would have created a national incident. And I was not worth that. The chaos would've thrown the country into…"

"No. It would have healed your country years earlier. Your mother could have exposed him for the madman that he was, and what purpose did it serve for her to protect him? All it did was protect her position as Queen. That's what it did. Your parents loved themselves more than they loved you, and on that score you're correct. But love isn't what created the brokenness in that scenario. It was the lack of it. Surely you must see that."

"In any case," he said, "I don't know how to love."

"That isn't true. You do know how to love… You do…"

"No. I am not the right man for that. I'm a broken vessel, and if you pour into me, it's all going to leak out, and I won't hold a drop of it in the end. I'm not worth it, Marissa."

"You're worth everything."

"No. No."

And then he stood and walked away from me, walked naked out of the bedroom, as if he weren't a king and we weren't in a palace full of other people. I knew the hallways would be empty, but still.

I ran out into the hall, without bothering with clothes myself, but I didn't see which way he'd gone.

Then I returned to the bed and sank to it in misery.

He didn't love me. He didn't want to love me.

And I had the feeling that something permanent had happened just now. That he had closed the door on something with a finality that would break us both.

I had given up on Hercules once, and I had cast him as the villain before. But I could see him now. See him for what he was. The wounded boy who was afraid.

Because his mother had offered him love but not protection.

Because she had given him words and not actions.

It scared me. Because my mother had been faithful to my father, she had demonstrated love every day, and she had given him as he asked, and he had taken advantage of it, and nothing had changed.

But I would have to trust that Hercules was a different manner of man, and that our love was different. That it could be bigger, that it could be better.

And that I could change him.

I knew that it was ludicrous. I knew that there were multiple self-help books on the topic.

But if he didn't want me, I was better off leaving. Demanding everything or taking nothing.

I would have to have faith. Faith in that first moment we had ever met.

In that certainty I had felt then.

I had lost that faith over the years, but when the truth had come out, it had become clear that Hercules hadn't been the villain.

And I had to trust it would bear out again.

But, oh, that trust would take a leap. The bravery to remain open when all I wanted to do was close in on myself...

I got beneath the covers, not caring that I was in his room. And I curled into a ball and dissolved.

Because in the morning I would have to emerge whole. I would have to do it for Lily, for Pelion and for the future of my marriage—such as it was.

But for the first time in my memory, the hope wasn't there. That little bubble had burst, abandoning me when I needed it most.

I had an answer to the question of what remained when you were plunged into darkness, what remained when the last vestige of hope was extinguished inside you.

It was love.

When everything else failed, love remained.

And that was simply where I would have to place my trust.

Because love never failed.

It was a truth that I believed, and it was one that I would hold to. I had no other choice.

CHAPTER FOURTEEN

Hercules

I HAD NOT spoken to Marissa in days. And I told myself that it was for the best. I told myself that I was doing the right thing.

Love.

She loved me. What did love mean?

Do people abandon you often?

The words that she had spoken to me stuck now, stung. I couldn't get them out of my head. They were like a barb in my heart.

I love you. My mother had said that, every time she had left the palace. Every time she had left me there.

But she had never taken me with her.

She loved me, but I was the heir.

She loved me, but I was Xerxes's son, not really hers.

I had been her obligation to the Crown, and I had given her freedom with my very existence.

That was why she loved me.

But she loved her freedom more, and she had gone her own way, flitting about the world as I was tortured.

Going about her life as I was broken and reshaped into a weapon for the throne of Pelion.

For my father's own satisfaction.

What good were words of love if there was nothing behind them?

What was wrong with a child that his mother could speak those words so carelessly and then leave him to be devoured by the wolves?

I didn't know.

I didn't understand.

All I knew was that those words felt like they had fractured something between us. Because they reminded me of the ache that I had felt in my soul when she had spoken them.

No.

I would not allow emotion, words, to create that kind of pain inside of me.

What could I reason? What could I see and touch? Certainly never my mother's love.

Those words were useless.

And yet I craved them.

For Marissa.

And I thought of Lily...

Lily, my own daughter, who I was avoiding like a true coward, because...

What if I gave her the words and failed miserably in the execution of them?

I didn't even know what love was supposed to look like.

The bloodline of my family was poison. And that was all it was. A bloodline, and not a family.

It was all I knew. All I understood.

I had taken to prowling the halls at night, because I couldn't sleep. My need for Marissa was like a sickness, and I didn't trust that I wouldn't go to her in a moment of weakness. This was what she had reduced me to. A man who did not trust himself. A man who wandered the halls of his own palace, questioning his sanity and trying to breathe around fractured pieces in his heart.

It was then I heard a sound. A whimpering sound, and I stopped for a moment, trying to figure out the source of it. It was the sound of a child, and for a moment that struck me as strange. Because for a moment, I could only think of myself.

I had whimpered like that in this palace, reduced to such a thing at the hands of my father. I couldn't move. Not then.

But I was jarred back to the present, and I knew it could not be me, for I was standing on my feet, and I was a man, not a child. And I was not helpless, which meant I had to move toward the sound, whatever it was.

I stopped at the door, and her name slammed into my mind.

Lily. Of course it was Lily.

I had been pushing her away in my mind, pushing Marissa away, and there she was, crying out.

And I could not turn away from her. That much I knew.

I pushed the door open slowly and saw her lying there in the bed, turning over and over fitfully, wrapping herself up in the blankets.

Her dark hair covered her eyes, and she looked distressed.

I crossed the room, feeling like anything but a king,

feeling like the lowest of men. Because I didn't know what to do, and none of my power, none of my money and none of my status would give me insight into what the best course of action should be.

But I couldn't abandon her.

"Lily," I whispered.

I went to the bed and sat on the edge, pressing my hand against her forehead. "Lily," I repeated.

"Daddy!" She sat upright and nearly crawled up my body, wrapping her arms around my neck. "Daddy. I dreamed that we were taken away from you. From here."

I was stunned into silence by that. That Lily's worst nightmare would be to be taken from here.

"I don't want to not know you," she said. "I remember when I didn't know you. It wasn't as good."

She clung to me with trust, this child, with helplessness and sadness, and I felt undone. Because who was I to deserve this?

She was so vulnerable…so helpless…

She felt her life was better for having me in it.

She didn't know. She didn't know who I was, how broken I was inside.

And she didn't care.

She loved me with an openness that had nothing to do with knowing me and everything to do with what I represented, and I kept thinking of what Marissa had said to me.

This was the love of a child.

A love so freely given, a love that didn't even have to be earned.

No, a love like this had to be stripped away.

And my parents had done that to me.

To me, when I had been like Lily.

When I would have happily crawled into either of their laps and offered them all my small heart.

Because that was what children did, and it was how they were made.

They came into the world with innocence, and it was taken.

"I can't sleep," she said.

"You haven't tried," I said.

"I know I can't. Will you sing me a song?"

"A song?" My heart thundered in my temples. "I don't sing."

"Everyone sings," she said matter-of-factly, and I didn't know how to argue with that.

I tried to think if I knew any songs that were suitable for children. The only thing that came to mind was something my nanny used to sing to me when I was a child. Back when I'd had a nanny...when there had been one soft person in my world.

The words were in Greek, so I clumsily tried to translate them along with the tune.

"Dear child, dear child, you've no need to cry.

Dear child, dear child, count the stars in the sky.

Dear child, dear child, rest your sleepy head.

Dear child, my child, rest in my heart.

For it is I who will love you even in your dreams."

"Promise?" she asked, her voice small and tired.

"I promise," I said.

And I meant it.

I would love her. I would protect her. I would fight armies for her.

And that no one had done it for me…

It was their failure, not mine.

To see myself through the eyes of a parent was… stunning.

My father had taken me when I was as young as Lily and put his hands on me to hurt me.

I touched Lily's cheek. I could not imagine harming her, let alone ordering that others harm her.

I would kill first. Anyone who dared harm a hair on her head.

My eyes felt dry.

Marissa had looked at me with trust and love once. And it was only there as I sat on the bed holding our daughter that I realized it.

The first time she saw me. A full acceptance of what was happening between us, even though it made no sense. Just implicit love. Implicit trust.

And I had thrown it back at her. She had been alone and pregnant, thrown out on her own. She had been wounded in my absence, and what had I done when I'd found her again? I had condemned her the same way so many others had.

And then…she had married me. She hadn't punished me by withholding Lily. She had given me my daughter, given me what I needed to run my country.

And then she had given me her body.

Given me her love.

I was suddenly overwhelmed by all this love that I knew for a fact I would never be able to earn.

This love that I wasn't being asked to earn.

Love.

I had been so convinced that it wasn't real, because I couldn't reason it out.

But that, I suddenly realized, was the beauty of love.

You might not be able to reason it out, but you could see it. You could touch it. You could feel it. And anything you couldn't see, touch and feel wasn't love. It was just words.

Hollow words that lacked any action.

And I was shamed, because I had not seen what was right before me. The gift that had been Marissa for the last five years.

When I was certain Lily was asleep, I dropped a kiss on her head, and I went down the hall.

I knew it was midnight. I knew that Marissa was probably sleeping, but this couldn't wait. It couldn't.

What good was being a king if you couldn't wake people up in the middle of the night when you were having an important revelation?

I didn't knock; I opened the door to her bedroom, and I realized that it couldn't be her bedroom anymore.

We needed a bedroom, together.

Because we were one, after all.

She and I had spoken of souls, and I had rejected the notion of them, but I knew now that they were real. And mine was tied with hers. The match, the mate. All manner of mystical things that I hadn't believed in before.

But didn't they come back to faith?

I had never believed I was a man of faith, but Marissa had shown me different.

"What are you doing here?" She was not asleep; she was perched on the edge of the bed in a white nightgown, looking confused. Though I imagined she had not been looking confused before I came into the room.

"We need to talk."

"It's after midnight."

"I know, but you are not sleeping."

"No. I haven't been. Not since…"

"I know," I said, moving to where she sat on the edge of the bed. Then I dropped to my knees, debasing myself for a second time in such a short period. But it would always be for them. For Marissa and Lily, and it would never be anything less than they deserved. For they were my life, my heart, my mission. And everything good that I did in the kingdom of Pelion would be an extension of that.

Of the love that existed between us.

"Lily had a nightmare," I said.

"Oh no. Is she okay?"

"She's fine. She's… She's beautiful. She's perfect. Marissa," I said, her name broken. "Marissa, I… I didn't realize. I didn't realize how love worked. I didn't realize how a child could love a parent, because I'd forgotten. I'd forgotten what it was like. They stole it from me. They tore it away from me, stripped it right out of my body. They hurt me. Abused me, abandoned me. And I thought something had to be broken in me, but when I looked down at Lily, so vulnerable and small and crying like that… The unspeakable wickedness of someone who could harm a child, who could tell them they love them and then leave them. It was not me. And you and Lily… You showed me what love really is. You are unwavering, Marissa. You gave me more than I've ever deserved. I sure as hell didn't earn it.

"All this grace that you bestowed upon me. This un-merited, unearned, unasked-for favor… It is like salva-tion, and I was too afraid to admit that I needed it. But I was in the darkness without you."

"Hercules… I… I have loved you, from the moment we met, but I'm sure that you loved me since then as well. I know you have."

"I have," I said, my voice rough. "I have loved you. It took hold of me that first day, and I didn't recognize it, because I didn't know a connection with women that was about something other than lust. What we had grew into lust, after we had a friendship, and I'd never ex-perienced anything like that. Someone who loved me after they knew me. Someone I wanted to speak to and sleep with in equal measure."

"You feel like your mother abandoned you," she said softly. "That's why it hurt you so much when you thought I'd left."

"I thought you cared about me. And I never put the two things together, because I did not think about my mother and her own fault in what had happened to me, because I could not bear to hate them both… But… Yes. That is why. Because I finally thought that someone cared for me again and then… And then that."

"I would never have left you," she said. "Believe that. And I won't now. No matter what. What we have is real. And it's worth fighting for. It's worth clinging to. Even if neither of us are perfect. Especially if neither of us are perfect. Because this was never about *perfect*. I grew up thinking that I had to be perfect. That I had to try to live up to this impossible thing. But my father left out grace. He left out joy. He left out love. And we'll fill our lives with that, surround ourselves with it."

"I never knew what it was, not really," I said, my voice rough. "But I would very much like to have a lifetime of discovering it with you."

"So would I," she said. "I knew that I found something special the first day I met you. And it scared me. Because I also knew that it would change everything. That you could ruin all of me. But I needed to be ruined. That old me, she needed to be ruined, so that I could be made whole."

"We will be whole together," I said. "I know that I told you I didn't believe in souls. That I didn't believe in things I could not see. But I see you. I see you, Marissa. And I feel that you love me. And I feel... I love you too. I have, from the beginning. I just didn't know what it was. I didn't know what to call it. I didn't know what to do with it."

"Neither did I," she said. "And I could never have known that we would end here. What a road that we walked. Separate for a while, but I'm ready to be together."

"And you know... With my father dead, we don't have to stay married. I have the throne. I have made Lily legitimate."

"You're not suggesting that we...get divorced."

"Never," I said. "But what I do want you to understand is that I'm not staying married to you for the bloodline. I'm not bound by anything. My country is not in peril. You are free to go, and I'm free to ask you to leave. But I won't ask that. I hope that you'll stay."

"You know I will," she said, scooting closer to me and grabbing hold of my face. "You know I will forever."

"I love you," I said.

And it was the first time I could ever remember saying those words to another person. "I love you," I said again. "And I love Lily." Suddenly, desperation filled my chest. "I need to go tell her."

She laughed. "No, you don't. It can wait until morning."

"It doesn't feel like it can. Everything feels desperate. So... I've never felt like this before. I love you. I love you so much."

"If it feels desperate, then perhaps we should explore that. Together."

And this time when she took me into her arms, and took me into her bed, it was not merely as lustful young people on a beach, not merely as husband and wife, but as a man and woman who were desperately in love.

And I knew that we would be that forever.

"I pledge myself to you," I said. "And I pledge to love you above all else."

"But you must love the country," she said.

"Everything good that I am comes from my love for you. My love for Lily stems from that, and what you taught me. My desire to be a good king in a richer, deeper sense than what my father was comes from loving you. I will love you above all others, above all else, for as long as I shall live."

"And I shall do the same."

EPILOGUE

Marissa

IT WAS A wonderful blessing, watching Hercules gaze at our son in the private nursing wing the day I gave birth. Lily was thrilled to have a little brother, and her excitement was difficult to contain. My mother had finally taken her home a few hours ago, exhausted. And that left Hercules and myself.

"I'm very glad that you got to see this. That you were part of it this time."

"So am I," he said, his voice rough as he gazed down at Leonidas.

Such a big name for such a tiny creature.

"You have a son."

"And a daughter," he said. "And I will protect both of them with every breath left in me. They will never question my love for them."

"No," I agreed, "they won't."

Our lives had been filled with love that no one on earth could ever question these past months. Hercules was the best King, the best husband, the best father. I was blissfully happy in a way I hadn't known it was possible to be. And it all seemed to just keep expanding.

That was the beautiful thing we were both discovering about love. It had no limits.

I looked at him, and I was cast back.

I'll never forget the first time I saw Prince Hercules, standing there on a beach.

Hercules, who was now King. Who bore a name fit for a god but who, blessedly for me, was a man. A man I loved.

And I never could have guessed that it would lead here, to a maternity ward in a hospital halfway across the world, to me being a queen, us being married, us being so blissfully in love neither of us could see straight.

I had been so certain he was my downfall. But in the end, I hadn't fallen. I had grown wings strong enough to fly. And now we flew together, my King and I.

It would be easy to call it fate, and perhaps whatever had brought us together was fate. But what kept us together was love. A love more powerful than all the pain the world had given to us.

And it was love that would sustain us.

Always.

* * * * *

LET'S TALK

Romance

For exclusive extracts, competitions
and special offers, find us online:

f facebook.com/millsandboon

⊙ @millsandboonuk

🐦 @millsandboon

Or get in touch on 0844 844 1351*

For all the latest titles coming soon,
visit millsandboon.co.uk/nextmonth